S0-AGL-933

THE TANGO PLAYER

Also by Christoph Hein

T H E   D I S T A N T   L O V E R

THE

Tango Player

CHRISTOPH HEIN

TRANSLATED BY PHILIP BOEHM

FARRAR, STRAUS & GIROUX

NEW YORK

Translation copyright © 1992 by Farrar, Straus and Giroux, Inc.
All rights reserved
Originally published in German under the title Der Tangospieler
copyright © 1989 by Christoph Hein
Published simultaneously in Canada by HarperCollinsCanadaLtd
Printed in the United States of America
Designed by Cynthia Krupat
First edition, 1992

Hein, Christoph.
[Tangospieler. English]
The tango player / Christoph Hein ; translated by Philip Boehm.—
1st ed.
Translation of: Der Tangospieler.
I. Title.
PT2668.E3747T3613   1992   91–17402 CIP
833'.914—dc20

This translation has been made possible in part by a grant
from the Wheatland Foundation, New York.

THE TANGO PLAYER

The day he was released Dallow couldn't move his fingers. They were stiff and cold and practically paralyzed. The prison officials handed him four papers to sign. Dallow wedged the pen between his thumb and forefinger and laboriously scrawled his signature.

"What's wrong with your hand?" asked the official who was sitting in front of him, watching.

"Nothing," answered Dallow. "The fear has crept into the bones of my fingers."

"You mean the excitement, don't you?"

"If I had meant that I would have said it."

The official looked at him and thought for a moment. Then he announced: "You'll have to see the doctor."

Dallow shook his head. "That's not necessary. My

fingers will be better in a few minutes. It's just a matter of ignoring the pain."

"Whatever you want. But in that case you need to sign this for me." He shoved another paper across the table. Dallow again wedged the pen between his fingers; the tip of his tongue jutted out as he drew his name on the paper. He examined his work: it resembled the signature of an eight-year-old. Satisfied, he nodded his head.

"What's your profession, Dallow?" asked the official. "It says here pianist, but in my files you're listed as assistant professor."

"Both are correct."

"That's no answer," the official replied patiently. "So what is your profession?"

"Pianist," said Dallow, "I came to you as a pianist and not as an assistant professor. Put down 'pianist.' "

Dallow stood in front of the desk and waited for permission to leave. His arms dangled at his sides, and the fingers of his right hand had turned completely white.

"Like the fingers of a wax saint," Dallow observed aloud.

The official looked up. He said nothing as he looked Dallow over, only shook his head wearily and let out an audible sigh.

As the door to the street was unlocked for him, Dallow asked the way to the train station. Clutching his satchel tightly, he set off in the direction indicated.

He didn't even look at the city in which he had been forced to reside for nineteen months. He knew he didn't like it; he couldn't like it. He was wearing a summer jacket and light-colored canvas shoes, and because it was February and icy-cold he was freezing.

At the train station he approached the window and asked for a ticket to Leipzig.

"Second class?" inquired the official.

"No, I travel first class," said Dallow.

"Then you'll have to wait two hours, because there's only second class on the ten-o'clock train."

"I can't wait."

Dallow bought a ticket and examined the departure times written by hand in black ink that had since faded, then entered the Mitropa station restaurant.

The waitress, an older woman who had tied a kitchen towel over her white apron, brought him some weak coffee and collected his money immediately. Dallow could see she knew where he had come from.

He bought cigarettes at the counter and smoked three in a row. He felt slightly dizzy. The sensation was not unpleasant.

He studied the few women seated among the men at the tables and tried to imagine sleeping with them. He had hoped this game would amuse him, but he didn't find any of the women attractive. He told himself it was stupid to expect anything better in a station restaurant before noon, especially on a cold February morning packed with dirty snow.

He glanced at the station clock above the exit, stood up, buttoned his coat, and went out. At the kiosk he bought two thin newspapers, one for news, one for sports—the only papers left.

Snow covered the steps to the underpass. Dallow slid his hand along the railing as he climbed down and then up again. He shivered.

The train arrived ten minutes late. Dallow boarded and sat down in an empty, dirty compartment that reeked of stale smoke. When he noticed that the car wasn't heated he stood up and walked through the train looking for a more pleasant place to sit. He wound up standing by a window in the corridor of a warm but overcrowded car. He read both papers, then stared out at the white landscape gliding by.

No one was waiting for him in Leipzig: he hadn't informed anyone he was coming. He had considered doing so, but then he couldn't think of anyone to tell. Still, he looked around the platform and then scanned the waiting area from the top of the stairs. He peered into the faces passing by.

In front of the station he approached a woman he didn't know and invited her to lunch. The girl—he assumed she was a student—was surprised. She gave him a thorough but friendly going-over, then turned and stepped away without a word. Dallow gazed after her with a vague feeling of regret. He did not feel offended.

He crossed the streetcar platform to the right of the station entrance and entered the Hotel Astoria. One of the waiters recognized him and showed him to a table.

"We haven't seen you for a while," he said as he handed Dallow the menu. Dallow nodded, took the waiter's recommendation, and ordered an entire bottle of wine. He looked around for familiar faces and was relieved to see only strangers. He tried to eat slowly; he was no longer in the habit and had to force himself not to rush. After the third glass of wine he began to feel the alcohol and ordered coffee.

An hour later he returned to the station and boarded the number 11 streetcar. Once again he checked for people he knew. At the same time he noticed various passengers staring at him. He guessed that his unseasonable clothes were to blame.

When they reached Dölitz he began watching the streets with greater interest. He was looking for changes; after his long absence he wanted to update his mental map of the familiar neighborhood where necessary. But nothing struck him as unusual, everything looked the same. When the streetcar stopped at the kindergarten, he got off and walked up the small side street to his apartment building. He unlocked the front door and turned on the light in the hallway. His mailbox was overflowing. He took out the newspapers and letters, then climbed the few steps to his apartment. As he opened the door he was relieved to find that both locks still worked. He also noticed he had chosen the right key for each lock without thinking.

He went into the bathroom, the kitchen, and both main rooms and opened all the windows. Then he tried to light the gas heaters. Apparently there was no gas in the pipes. He had to let each unit run a long time before any gas that could be lit began to flow. He turned up the thermostats as high as they would go. Then he shut all the windows. He went into the kitchen and turned on the faucet until the water ran clear. He opened the coffee tin. Although the coffee inside seemed darker than usual he spooned a little into a pot and put some water on to boil. He opened the pantry, the refrigerator, the cupboard, took out what few provisions he could find and sniffed at them. Where necessary, he also tasted them, carefully, skeptically. Anything questionable he dropped into the garbage pail, which was overgrown with layers of black and white mold.

The dust attracted his attention. He noticed it first on the cupboard, then on the black piano and all the other furniture. A dust so fine it was invisible until he slid his fingers over the wood.

He brewed the coffee and crossed into the living room carrying the pot and a cup. He unbuttoned his coat but didn't take it off. He poured himself some coffee. Then he sat down and skimmed through his letters. Two were from the building management, one from the electric company. He looked over the remaining envelopes without opening them.

The newspapers were from the twenty-fourth to the thirty-first of October. He concluded that Rita must have left on the twenty-third or the morning of the twenty-fourth. He leafed through the old papers. He had the impression that the news they contained was less important than the papers claimed, even then.

He felt warm. He took off his coat, walked into the bathroom and lit the stove for the bath. He crumpled up single sheets of newsprint, stuffed them into the firebox, and added whatever firewood he could find in the coal bin. Later, lying in the bathtub, he read letters whose entire charm consisted in their having reached him so late. Each time he finished one he would fold it into a little ship and launch it in the tub.

After lying in bed for an hour—he slept poorly because the room was quickly overheated and in his sleep he kept hearing the clang of iron doors—he got up, went to the wardrobe, and picked out some fresh underwear and a suit. Once dressed, he had the feeling he was wearing a costume, a feeling he confirmed by glancing at the long mirror in the wardrobe. Habits change quickly, he thought, and tied his tie.

Suddenly he tore open all the dresser doors and rummaged through the shelves inside. He tried to figure out which of his things Rita took when she moved out eighteen months earlier and sent him a short letter announcing her departure. At the time he had merely spat, crumpled the page, and resolved not to waste another thought on her.

He broke off the search as suddenly as he had begun. He realized it was futile. He could barely remember what things he owned. His hunt for missing goods only uncovered objects that surprised and confused him, objects he had long forgotten and which he now contemplated in a vain attempt to retrace how he had acquired them in the first place.

He sat down, then stood up immediately to look for a key in his desk drawer. He left the apartment and crossed through the basement to the garages along the courtyard. He unlocked one of the doors and switched on the light. There was his car, with one flat tire and covered with dust. He opened the door, seated himself behind the wheel and tried to start the engine. As he expected, nothing happened. He sat for a while in his car, caressed the steering wheel, shifted the gears and pushed various buttons. He leaned back and smiled.

"I missed you," he said to his car, "women and you."

He opened the hood, replenished the water in the battery, and hooked it up to the charger, all the while taking care not to dirty his suit. Then he locked the garage and returned to his apartment. He washed his hands thoroughly. Afterward he put on his winter coat and wool cap and went out. He didn't see a single neighbor as he walked to the stop to catch the street-car back into the city.

Once downtown, he walked past the opera up Grimmaische Strasse to the Thomaskirchhof. He strolled along Petersstrasse, watching people and studying the window displays. His pace was so slow that he was shunted aside several times. The women were thickly bundled up and moving hurriedly, he saw little more of them than their eyes.

He paused in front of the cinema to look at the pictures on display and to read the local movie guide. The titles meant nothing to him; he was pleased to see they were all new. The unknown films promised entertainment. He now felt that something had, after all, changed in the twenty-one months he was away.

He walked down Schlossgasse to the Dittrichring and entered the café where Harry worked. All the tables were taken. He crossed the lower room and climbed the few steps that led to the bar upstairs. Here, too, everything was taken. At the one large table in the café he noticed his lawyer. He walked over, and it wasn't until he was standing directly in front of him that Dallow realized his judge was there as well. His lawyer seemed nervous when Dallow said hello. He stood up, shook hands, and asked how Dallow was doing. Dallow only nodded and smiled.

Because the others at the table had broken off their conversation and all were staring his way, the lawyer felt compelled to introduce his former client.

"We've already met," Dallow said to the judge, "you are Dr. Berger."

"That's right," replied the man. "Unfortunately I can't recall—"

"You sentenced me a year and a half ago," interrupted Dallow.

"Dallow, Dallow," the judge repeated. He thought a moment.

"Twenty-one months," said Dallow, trying to help, "including detention pending investigation . . ."

Now the judge remembered. "That's right, I saw your file on my desk just a few days back. You want to speak to me?"

Dallow shook his head.

"What do you want, then?" continued the judge, now a little louder. "Do you feel you were treated unfairly? Do you have claims to make? In that case you should have my office set an appointment. Go see my secretary."

"I have nothing to say to you," answered Dallow.

"Then why did you track me down here? Why are you following me around?" exclaimed the judge incredulously.

"I have nothing to say to you," Dallow repeated, "I saw Herr Kiewer and wanted to say hello."

Dr. Berger huffed and reached for his glass. Herr

Kiewer, the defense lawyer, was at a loss whether he should remain standing next to Dallow or sit back down beside the judge. Distractedly he told Dallow they should get together sometime, clapped him on the shoulder, and returned to the judge.

Dallow walked over to the bar. He did not recognize the bartender. When she turned to wait on him he ordered some coffee and asked about Harry.

"He's not here," she said, "but he's on this evening."

She was wearing a loose-fitting silk dress that buttoned down the front. Her hair was pinned up and didn't seem particularly clean. Her heavily made-up hollow cheeks aroused more pity in Dallow than interest. He guessed she was a little over thirty. She looks cheap, he thought.

As she handed him his coffee she said, "Harry's here now. He's up with the boss."

"Thanks," said Dallow. He sat down on a barstool that had just been vacated, turned his back to the bar, and observed the clientele. His eyes avoided the table where his judge and lawyer were sitting. At two other tables he saw faces that appeared familiar, but his efforts to place them were in vain. He noticed he was the only guest wearing a suit. And since he wasn't used to wearing one and, since it was uncomfortable, the feeling of being inappropriately dressed grew even more intense. He turned back to the bar. The two men sitting next to him were arguing loudly about politics. He glanced at them briefly, at their young, immature faces. Students, thought Dallow, and smiled wryly.

He continued to eye the bartender. He ordered wine and a second coffee. He kept on looking at the buttons of her dress, at her breasts. She smiled back and he looked down at his hands. She took the empty glasses from the bar and let them drop into the sink.

"What's the matter with you?" she asked quietly. "Haven't you ever seen a woman before?"

Dallow looked up. The woman was bending over the sink, rinsing the glasses. For a minute he was unsure whether she was addressing him.

"As a matter of fact I have, but it's been a long time," he answered, just as quietly. She glanced at him and continued thrusting the glasses into the water. "Well?" she asked. "How do I rate?"

"I don't know yet."

His answer surprised her. "You don't know," she said. "What is it you need to know?"

"I meant to say I haven't made up my mind."

The woman looked at him with contempt. She shook her head abruptly, somewhat peeved.

"Why don't you finish your wine and leave me alone."

She went to the refrigerator and took out an ice tray. She pried the ice cubes loose with a knife. Undeterred, Dallow continued to watch her breasts. The two men next to him were still arguing about Prague and Dubček. They were so loud that Dallow felt they were disturbing his study of the bartender's breasts.

A waiter came through the swinging door that led to the kitchen. He stood next to Dallow and reviewed the customers, a cigarette stuck in the corner of his mouth. Like the other waiters, he was wearing a burgundy-colored tuxedo, but his was so old that parts of it actually glistened. It also seemed too small and tight over his disproportionately large stomach.

"Hello, Harry," said Dallow without getting up.

It took the waiter a few seconds to recognize him. Then he placed his arm on Dallow's shoulder by way of greeting.

"How long have you—"

"This morning," Dallow cut him off.

"And how was it?" asked the waiter after a moment's hesitation, during which he seemed to be searching for the right words.

"I've already put it out of my mind," said Dallow and smiled at the waiter. "Lost time, not worth the trouble trying to remember."

Harry nodded in agreement.

"And what's new here?"

The waiter thought for a minute and then brushed the question aside with a vague, ambiguous shrug.

"You've gotten fat, Harry."

The waiter grimaced. "I suspect I've eaten a little better than you have in recent years."

Dallow agreed.

"Who's the girl? I don't know her."

"Christa, the boss's daughter. The old man threw out three girls in a row for cheating him. Now he's handed the bar over to his daughter, except she doesn't have the faintest idea about running a business. I had to teach her everything, dumb woman. The only thing she's really good at is going to bed with her customers and putting the lie on her old man. And he doesn't notice, or else he pretends he doesn't."

He spoke quietly and smiled at the bartender.

Then he turned to Dallow and grinned: "At the moment, she's exactly what you need." Since Dallow didn't answer, he asked, "You want a table?"

Dallow nodded.

"Just wait and something will free up in a minute. Today it's all on me. You're my guest."

He patted Dallow on the back.

"And Rita?" he asked. "What's she up to?"

"I don't know," said Dallow, "I haven't seen her since. She left me right after the trial."

"Women," muttered the waiter disapprovingly, "it's always the same."

"I'm not shedding any tears over her," said Dallow sourly.

Harry nodded.

"That's right. It's not worth it." After a pause he asked: "Was it really bad—in there?"

"I'm still alive," said Dallow calmly.

The waiter nodded again. He leaned over and added: "I always told you anyone who plays the piano as bad as you do has got to wind up in jail sooner or later."

He laughed heartily at his own joke. Then he gave Dallow a rap on the shoulder and made his rounds, greeting various guests with a handshake and taking their orders. He stopped to say something at the large round table where the judge was sitting with Dallow's lawyer. Since the men all laughed aloud and looked his way, Dallow guessed that Harry had repeated his joke. Dallow turned back to the bar and finished his wine.

Fifteen minutes later Harry showed him to a small table that had become free. A woman who plopped down in a seat opposite him annoyed Dallow with her monosyllabic answers and unfriendly silence. She soon let herself be led away by one of her dancing partners. Dallow observed the judge, who seemed slightly inebriated. He was amazed that the man now resembled a happy, pudgy burgher who tended his garden on the weekend and polished his car. During the proceedings, two years earlier, he had seemed cool, exaggeratedly correct, and zealous. Dallow noticed the judge's hunched back, the poorly shaved hair on his neck, his large reddish ears and he recalled the stupid irony with which the judge had posed his questions.

Shortly before midnight Dallow attempted to pay his tab, but Harry wouldn't allow it and repeated that Dallow was his guest. They said goodbye several times. Harry accompanied him to the coat room and Dallow had to promise he would come back soon. He rode the streetcar home and went straight to bed.

Dallow spent the whole next day in the garage working on his car. He checked out the engine, reconnected the battery, changed one of the tires, and cleaned the car. Around noon he stopped to go to the bank, buy groceries, and have a meal in one of the small pubs near the fairgrounds.

It was getting dark when he finally managed to start the car and pull out onto a street gouged by rails and pockmarked by frost. He drove out of the city. Just outside of Wachau he parked the car by a small forest. He tried to enter the woods, but so much snow fell on him from the dense, drooping pine trees that he quickly gave up after a few steps. He walked along the highway at the edge of the forest. Whenever a car passed he stepped onto the snow-covered shoulder of the road, and turned his face away to avoid being blinded by the oncoming traffic. The cold air turned his cheeks and nose red. When he came to the end of the small wood he felt the icy wind and turned around. He returned to his car, then repeated the same walk to the end of the wood. Again and again he paced back and forth along the same stretch of road. He wanted to resolve the many uncertainties, the vague, indefinite thoughts that constantly preoccupied him but which he couldn't even begin to formulate.

In the past twenty-one months he had thought about himself incessantly. The cramped cell, the limited distractions, the reduced human contact, the strictly regulated daily routine that knew no exceptions or surprises had forced him to focus on himself time and again, at first unconsciously, and later in clear opposition to his will. He soon noticed that his reflections traveled in circles. There was no sensible conclusion; none of his musings had any practical consequence, and so they inevitably became confused, and he soon lost the ability to express them in words. His thinking was incomplete; it filled his head with a strange, impenetrable, and disconcerting jumble of fractured ideas. Occasionally a particular thought seemed full of promise, and he would embrace it ardently only to then sink back into his original despair—perhaps because he had deceived himself, perhaps because he had been overly enthusiastic, or perhaps because he had simply lost his capacity for logic, for carefully thinking something through to a useful end. He decided to postpone all reflection until after his release. Still, he was often overcome by the fear of going insane.

And now he was free and the only resolution that

seemed clear and obvious to him was the decision to forget the past months as rapidly as possible. He didn't want to think about them, much less talk about them. He wanted to erase this time from his memory so he could free himself from it. He had never been able to view his imprisonment as a punishment, only as an annoyance, an irreplaceable loss of time. But he had managed to get through the two years without losing his mind, and from now on he refused to waste a single minute on senseless brooding over his imprisonment and the degrading conditions he had had to endure.

His shoes were soon soaked through, and he felt the cold pinching his ears.

After twenty-one months all he could feel was a huge deafening emptiness in his head. He was at a loss, this thought kept swirling through his mind, and he felt as if a metal string had been plucked inside his brain and the dull, unremitting note was droning against his skull. He was afraid he was losing his hearing.

He returned to his car and climbed in. The engine ran smoothly on the way home and made him happy. His machine had survived the two years of involuntary rest unscathed. It ran without a hitch, reliably. Exemplary, thought Dallow, I should take my car as an example.

At home he changed shoes. Then he stood in front

of the mirror and combed his hair for a long time. Afterward he checked his supply of cash and pulled on his coat. He rode the streetcar downtown. It was almost ten o'clock when he walked into a hotel night-club, slipped a waiter some money, and was shown to a table. The music was very loud, and Dallow had trouble making things out in the dim room hung with colored lights.

An hour after midnight he accompanied a young woman home to her apartment. A four-year-old was lying on a mattress in the hallway; the child awoke as they entered.

"Go back to sleep" said the woman and ran her hand through the child's hair.

She quickly led Dallow to the main room so she could turn out the hall light and close the door.

"Why is your child sleeping in the hall?" asked Dallow.

The young woman blushed: "It's just for tonight. Usually we both sleep here in the main room. I don't like to put the bed in the kitchen on account of the gas stove."

Dallow nodded. There was something else he wanted to ask, but he noted he was no longer able to articulate it. Everything was unclear, blurred. He dropped onto the bed and asked the young woman to undress him.

When he woke up the next morning she was saying

goodbye. He spoke without opening his eyes. He wanted to avoid looking at the woman with whom he had spent the night.

"Are we going to see each other tonight?" she asked.

Dallow mumbled a sleepy answer.

"There's a key on the kitchen table," she said, "you can keep it if you want to come back. Otherwise lock the door and drop the key through the mail slot."

On the other side of the door the child started shouting.

"I have to go," said the woman, "I hope I'll see you again."

Without opening his eyes, Dallow gave another indefinite and unintelligible answer. When he heard the door open he tried to catch a glimpse of the woman. He watched her leave, he saw her back, her behind, her legs. He closed his eyes, satisfied, relieved. When he heard the outside door click shut, he stood up. He went to the window and looked out. He could see a courtyard, a few trees, a bar for beating carpets, and large square garbage bins. He ran to the kitchen and stood sideways at the window to avoid being seen. He didn't have to wait long. The young woman and her child were crossing the street. When she reached the sidewalk she stopped and looked back up at her apartment. Dallow pulled in his head. He waited for a second, then leaned back out and watched her until she and the child disappeared from sight.

Not bad, she's not bad at all, he said to himself and smiled.

He went through the apartment inspecting the rooms. He put on a robe he found in the bathroom. Since his bare feet were cold he forced them into the small, fur-lined slippers lying in front of the tub. He went to the kitchen to eat breakfast. He found a hard-boiled egg wrapped in a kitchen towel, some coffee in a thermos. Dallow enjoyed sitting down at a table someone had set. And he enjoyed being alone at that moment.

The doorbell rang several times. Dallow stayed seated and kept still. When he heard steps in the stair-well he stood up and went into the hallway. A tele-gram was lying at the foot of the door. He picked it up, placed it on the kitchen table in front of him, and continued eating his breakfast. Then he lit a cigarette and searched, unsuccessfully, for an ashtray. Finally he tapped his ashes into the empty eggshell. He reached for the telegram. "Elke Schütte," he read aloud. He tried to read it without opening it. He failed, and put the telegram back on the table. Then he stubbed out his cigarette and took a sharp knife out of a drawer. He discreetly pried open the tele-gram, careful not to tear the paper. He read: ARRIVE EIGHT P.M., YOURS RUDOLF. He placed the text back in the envelope, moistened the flap, and pressed it shut. Then he dropped the telegram on the floor in the hallway so that it once again lay by the door. He washed up. A fresh towel and a piece of soap still in the wrapper were lying on top of the washing machine. A ceramic cup contained a toothbrush packed in cellophane. Dallow liked being cared for this way. He opened the doors of the medicine cabinet, took out the jars and glass bottles, and checked their contents. He closed his eyes to savor the aromas. In one drawer he found a razor. He picked it up, amused. Is it Rudolf's, he thought, or is it for Elke's legs, or for guests like me?

After he finished dressing, he left the apartment and locked the door. He wanted to drop the key into the mail slot, but he hesitated, unlocked the apartment and went back in. He tore a piece of paper from a pad, sat down at the kitchen table and wrote: I'll drop by soon some evening. I'm keeping the key. I kiss you, P.

He read the message and thought for a minute. Then he spelled out his full name at the bottom, Hans-Peter Dallow, and wrote down his phone number. He realized he hadn't used his telephone since returning to the city, and because he was unsure that it was still connected, he added: The phone rarely works. He placed the note on top of the telegram by the door. Then he bent down and laid the telegram on top of his note. That seemed to be the more proper sequence. He went out and locked the door, taking the key with him.

Once inside the streetcar, he noted Elke's name and

address in his calendar. He wondered whether the child was a boy or a girl. He tried to recall its voice, but he was unsure. He remembered the child had woken up when he and Elke passed through the hall, but he hadn't really paid attention. In any case, he couldn't remember. And when he had watched them from the kitchen window he had focused only on the woman.

Back in his apartment he put on a fresh shirt. Then he went to the telephone and lifted the receiver. He heard the dial tone. He held the phone close to his ear and wondered whether it had been disconnected or whether it had continued to ring throughout his twenty-one months in jail—assuming, of course, that someone had tried to call. The thought amused him. Then he dialed a number, no number in particular, and listened to the ringing with satisfaction. Before he could hang up, a voice rattled off something impossible to understand. Dallow was surprised. He didn't want to speak with anyone, he had only wanted to check whether his phone worked.

"Dallow. Who is this, please?" he finally said.

"Who is *this* you mean?" countered the unfriendly male voice.

"Dallow," he said, "this is Hans-Peter Dallow."

For a moment there was silence. Then the voice said: "Peter? Is that you, Peter?"

"Yes," said Dallow. "With whom am I speaking?"

"It's Jürgen, Jürgen Roessler," said the voice.

Dallow realized that he had unconsciously dialed his old number at the Institute. Roessler inquired awkwardly how Dallow was getting along and asked whether he wanted to see him. They agreed to meet.

Dallow hung up, amazed at himself. He had made a date with Roessler without really wanting to. He had nothing to say to him. But he had nothing else to do either, and he was curious. He wanted to see Roessler's face, he wanted to hear him try to explain things. For that pleasure he would gladly sacrifice an hour of his time.

He sat down at the desk and looked through the papers and statements he had picked up at the bank the day before. His account didn't show too many changes: monthly rent payments, electricity charges, and postal service fees, that was all. His last paycheck had been deposited three days after his arrest. The only subsequent income came from interest on his account. He was amused to realize he could live an entire month off the interest alone.

The phone rang just as he was leaving the apartment. He answered quickly. He waited anxiously for the caller to speak, the first person to call after his long absence.

"This is Schulze," said a man's voice, "Schulze from the Municipal Council. I'd like to talk to you, Herr Dallow."

"You are talking to me," said Dallow, disappointed.

The caller laughed. "It would be good if we could meet."

"About what?" asked Dallow.

"I would prefer to tell you in person. Is two o'clock all right with you?"

Dallow hesitated. "I really don't know why we should . . ."

"I'll explain when you come. At two o'clock, then, all right? Check in with the doorman at the District Court when you arrive. It's right behind your former Institute. You know it, don't you? We'll be waiting for you there.

"In the District Court?" asked Dallow, astonished.

"That's right, that's right," the caller laughed, "we rent some of the rooms there. You know how it is, never enough bureaus for the bureaucracy."

He laughed again loudly, jovially. Then he said, "So we'll see you at two, Herr Dallow," and hung up.

Dallow stood holding the receiver, wondering. "I never said I'd meet you," he shouted into the phone.

Half an hour later, he drove into town.

He ran into some students as he was entering the building where his former Institute took up the entire second floor. He observed them closely, but didn't recognize a single one. He climbed the stone steps and was almost knocked over by all the young people. When he opened the door to the inside stairwell, he saw Sylvia. She was leaning against the railing, talking to a young man with a beard. Dallow stopped and observed her. He still found her attractive. He went up to her, put his arm around her shoulder, and greeted her with a kiss on the cheek.

"Did you survive everything all right?" she asked.

He nodded. Some students were coming downstairs and he stepped aside to let them pass.

"How about getting some coffee?" he asked.

The bearded man said goodbye. Sylvia shook her head and said she had to go to a seminar. She smiled, and Dallow looked at her searchingly. He wanted to sleep with her at once. He wanted to slide his hand inside her thick coat and under her clothes, right there, on the stairs, at the university, he wanted to caress her breasts, stroke her skin, and then go with her somewhere right away, undress her, and go to bed with her. He stared at the small white bit of her neck peeking out from underneath her woolen scarf. Twenty-one months, he thought, that should be amusing for her too.

"Seminar?" he said absently. "I thought you'd be through with your studies by now."

Sylvia smiled and nodded.

"Oh, I see," he said. "I'm sorry I missed your exams. I would have made sure you passed, Sylvia. I would have given you the best grades. In every subject, the best possible grades."

"I know," she said and pushed him back a little with her index finger, "but you're mistaken. I *am* through with my studies. I've been an assistant for over a year now. And I'm teaching this seminar for the third semester. Are you surprised?"

"Yes," confessed Dallow, "I hadn't expected that. You're actually working on your doctorate? And all those years I had my hands full making sure you even passed. Who's my lucky successor? Not Roessler, I hope. Such a good family man? That's not your style, Sylvia."

Her smile turned very cool. Dallow beamed at her, but it was difficult to hide his disappointment. You just have to get used to the idea, he told himself, life went on without you. No one waited around for you, and you can't simply pick up where you left off.

"But then again, why not," he said, "you always were the most beautiful girl in the school. Why shouldn't you become an assistant. It never occurred to me, and yet it's so obvious."

She pursed her lips lightly. "Just as arrogant as ever," she said pointedly. "It probably also never occurred to you that I might have other abilities."

Dallow only replied, "But, Sylvia." He said it as sweetly and as maliciously as he could. He felt rejected and hurt and wanted to hurt her back.

"I have to go," she answered and turned toward the stairs.

He explained that he wanted to talk to Roessler and could accompany her upstairs.

"Do you want to start here again?" she asked.

"I don't know," answered Dallow, "I haven't thought about it yet. I just want to hear what Roessler has to say. After all, I worked here for years."

"Shall I put in a good word for you?"

Dallow laughed. "You're absolutely right—it's come to that. Yes, I suppose you could put in a good word for me. It's a crazy world, isn't it Sylvia?"

"I suppose that depends on who's looking at it," said Sylvia very reservedly.

"Everything always depends on who's looking at it," said Dallow. "Subjective point of view, I remember."

He walked her to the door of her classroom. It was open, a few students were standing in the hall, smoking. Upon Sylvia's arrival, they put out their cigarettes and went inside. Sylvia said goodbye to Dallow and wished him well in his talk with Roessler.

Dallow smiled and replied: "You know I couldn't keep you out of my mind for the past twenty-one months? I kept dreaming about you, Sylvia, for twenty-one whole months."

Since she didn't respond, he continued: "And do you know why?"

"I can imagine," she said slowly and ironically. "I've heard about male fantasies in lonely cells. I'm not sure how flattered I should feel."

Dallow took her by the arm. "We were supposed to get together the evening I was arrested. I was supposed to go to your place. Have you forgotten? Didn't you miss me when I didn't show up?"

He saw that she was thinking, confused.

"You had invited me to a pajama party that evening. Three of your girlfriends were going to come along with some men I didn't know. Unfortunately I was detained. It's a real pity. I've often thought about that party. I tried to picture it. I can imagine it was a lot of fun."

"I'm afraid you're confusing things, sweetheart," said Sylvia, freeing her arm from his grasp. She wanted to leave but he blocked the entrance to the classroom.

"No, Sylvia, that's impossible. I haven't been invited to very many parties in the last two years. Do you still have pajama parties? I'd really like to come to one. When you've thought about something like that as long as I have, you really want to put the theory to a practical test. That's my current scientific ambition, Sylvia."

"I'm sorry, Peter. I really don't know what you're talking about. But why don't you talk to some of the cute little students. They might be delighted to throw a party like that just for you. And now you'll have to excuse me, but I'm already late for my seminar."

She pushed him aside, stepped into the room and vigorously shut the door behind her. Dallow remained standing outside the closed door. He heard Sylvia's voice calling out names and asking questions, a little too loudly. He found her voice unpleasant. He recognized the pedantic intonation from his own seminars. He recognized the tired condescension with which he had listened to his students, occasionally nodding or rolling his eyes at the feeblemindedness he was forced to endure. He recalled the contempt he had felt as he doled out praise, as he kindly collected assignments or respectfully accepted a week's work. The questions they would ask, year after year, the naïve, quaint questions about all the world's riddles. Every sentence a testimony of faith, an unbridled hope, poised for enlightenment, awaiting a fundamental explanation. And his answers, which had to be equally radiant and lofty if he wanted to be understood. To speak from experience didn't help; it tended to irritate, to sound resigned, cynical. So he kept his sarcastic comments to himself and nodded, his eyes as wide and bright as his students'. The corners of his mouth hurt from his constant twinkling smile. What discipline and care it took for him to submit to such stupidities year after year. And what arrogance. Dallow stood at the door and listened quietly. Then he went to see Roessler.

Barbara Schleider, the Institute's secretary, greeted him at the reception area. She stood up when he entered, walked over to him and grabbed hold of his head with both hands.

"It's nice to see you back," she said and pulled his head down to kiss him on the forehead.

Dallow was moved and flustered and leaned his forehead against her breast.

"I think you're the only one who's really glad I'm out," he said.

"You're right, not everybody's overjoyed," she replied and shot a glance at the door of the adjoining room.

She returned to her seat, took some cigarettes from her desk and offered him one.

"What happened while I was gone?" asked Dallow. "What did you do without me?"

"Nothing," she answered, "nothing happened. I just got a little more beautiful, that's all."

"I noticed that when I came in. I'm wondering whether I shouldn't marry you."

"I'm sorry but you know I prefer men with big sailboats. It's good for the complexion."

"I can see that, Barbara."

She beamed at him, and Dallow asked himself whether this woman really wasn't just right for him. She was a few years older than him, although you couldn't tell by looking at her. He appreciated well-groomed women; experience had taught him they were more subtle and less obtrusive. If I ever do marry again, he thought, I really should marry Barbara.

"But big sailboats . . . that sounds like older gentlemen. Aren't you missing something?"

"When I want to relax, I appreciate being left in peace."

"Then I'm afraid we'll never make a couple. When

I think of you lying there, sunning yourself, and your men can't come up with anything better than to leave you in peace—they really must be ancient, these gentlemen."

"And you really must have been pretty lonely lately."

"You're right. Imagine, even the nurses in the clinic were men."

Dallow had sat down at her desk and was playing with her pencils. Neither noticed when the door to the next room opened and Roessler appeared. He greeted Dallow and invited him in.

"Would you like some coffee?" he asked, and when Dallow nodded he asked the secretary to bring two cups. Then he closed the door.

Dallow took a seat in one of the armchairs before Roessler had a chance to offer him one.

It's true, nothing has happened, thought Dallow as he studied the room, the old warped window frames, the curtains cut from some cheap material that always seems to gather dust, the glass case with stack after stack of red brochures, the color photographs above the door, Roessler's desk as neat as ever, the green writing pad placed exactly in the middle of the dark brown surface. Dallow's former desk was also still around, though it was backed into a corner now and used more as a dumping place for books and files.

Roessler stopped in front of Dallow's chair.

"Excuse me, but do you mind if I ask you not to smoke?"

"Of course not," said Dallow and held his burning cigarette up high. "Do you have an ashtray?"

"You'll have to use Barbara's."

Dallow went out. As he was putting out his cigarette, he whispered to the secretary, "Asshole."

"You can say it out loud, he knows he is," she said without looking up.

Dallow listened in silence to Roessler's intricate greeting. He immediately recalled the man's predilection for drawn-out introductions and watched him closely, fascinated by what he saw.

"And now what can I do for you?" Roessler finally asked.

Dallow hadn't been listening and kept nodding his head in agreement until he realized this was a question he was supposed to answer.

"What is it you expect from me?" Roessler repeated himself.

Dallow spread his arms in a gesture of helplessness. "I don't know," he said.

Roessler stared in surprise at Dallow, who sat silently in the cheaply upholstered armchair, painting invisible figures on the table. Then he leaned back and waited for a response.

Dallow wondered what to ask. But the only question on his mind was why he had come here in the first place. He continued drawing geometric figures with growing intensity. Then he said, unexpectedly, "Congratulations."

Roessler looked at him, puzzled. Dallow pointed to the desk without saying a word.

"Thank you," said Roessler, blushing with embarrassment. "Well, the professorship became available and you were not at our disposal."

Dallow nodded happily. "No I wasn't. In fact, you might say I had been disposed of."

Roessler waited, then patiently repeated his question: "You wanted to see me?"

"The coffee's very good," replied Dallow.

Roessler eyed him in complete bewilderment. "What is it you want?" he finally asked. "Do you want to work here again?"

"I don't know," replied Dallow, without interrupting his play on the tabletop.

Roessler shook his head. "That wouldn't be a good idea. At the time, we drew up papers for terminating your contract by mutual consent. That was to your advantage. Now you'd have to apply all over again, which takes time. And I have no idea whether they'll agree. There aren't any openings. And besides, people will wonder whether we can expose our students to a man who . . ."

Dallow looked up with interest and waited for him to finish the sentence. But since Roessler apparently couldn't find the right words, Dallow supplied them: "Who is a criminal."

"No, I didn't say that," Roessler broke in sharply.

"Then, perhaps, a former criminal," suggested Dallow politely.

"Don't be absurd. The whole affair was stupid and that's exactly what I told the court, as you know. It wasn't exactly a brilliant performance on your part, but sending you to prison was an unnecessary over-reaction. Those were hectic times, everywhere you looked people were turning up enemies and reacting hysterically. Today things would be different. You'd receive an official reprimand and that's all. We've made some progress since then. But at the time, well, you know yourself."

Dallow nodded.

"And if you want my advice, Peter, the best thing for you to do is forget it all. Forget the whole dumb thing. Of course it won't be easy, but that would be the best way of making a completely new start. Forget what happened and focus on the future."

Dallow was now drawing circles and spirals and trying to make sense of the words he was hearing. The word "future" startled him. It sounded so significant, but he couldn't imagine what it might mean. He would have liked to ask Roessler, but at the same time he realized Roessler wouldn't understand the question and would feel that Dallow was goading him.

And he had the vague impression that all his problems—his inability to think, his brooding, his general sense of being at a loss—were tied to this very word. His future seemed like an enormous sheet of paper, white and terrifying. If he could only draw a few lines on it, no matter how indefinite and blurred they might be, it would help him think clearly, at least he would be able to formulate a thought, a simple, normal thought.

But why, he asked, was he evidently the only one who had this difficulty, and no one else? Why did this particular word cripple his brain? Dallow continued drawing lines and circles on the table, relentlessly. Presumably, he said to himself, the future is simply an extension of what has already happened or what is now taking place. Roessler only needs to go on doing what he's been doing day after day, he only has to keep sitting in his chair and his future is certain, bright and clear. But for Dallow, even simple continuity was a problem. If he were still in his cell today he would have as clear and certain a future as Roessler, if not quite as comfortable. But the prison had released him, that past was finished. He couldn't draw any lines connecting it with that big empty paper on which his future would reveal itself. He had no past, no place to start from, nothing that would allow a continuation, nothing that would spare him future choices by dictating one single natural choice.

"Without a past there is no future," he said aloud.

And then he smiled, because he remembered saying this sentence in the lectures and seminars back then, in that past that lay behind his current past. He had always pronounced this sentence with the required pathos, but not until now did its true meaning dawn on him.

He looked up and noticed Roessler staring at him with concern—concern and mistrust. In order to reassure him, Dallow repeated the sentence as dramatically as if he had just discovered its wisdom: "You don't have a future without a past."

Roessler seemed to want to ignore the remark. With a patience that caused him visible strain, he dropped his folded hands on the desk and nodded, resigned.

"So shall I call Berlin?" he asked wearily.

Dallow then realized what Roessler had been saying the whole time: that he couldn't employ Dallow in his institute but that he could use his connections in Berlin.

Dallow shook his head. "No," he said, "I still don't know what I'm going to do."

Roessler was utterly baffled: "What do you mean you don't know? You had one and a half years to think about it. You had all the time in the world to think about that and nothing else. And now you don't know? What did you do your whole time in prison? Write a novel?"

"I did think about it. I thought about it every day,"

protested Dallow vehemently, "but I still don't know the answer."

The two men stared at one another with hostility. Both were annoyed, and each suspected he was being used—or abused—by the other.

"Is there anything else I can do for you?" Roessler finally asked and with this question let Dallow know once and for all there was nothing else he could or would do for him and that he considered their conversation over.

Dallow stayed in his seat out of spite and tried to create the impression that he was seriously considering Roessler's question, that he was concerned to help Roessler find the answer. But a moment later he looked up at the clock and said he had to go to another appointment. Each thanked the other for the conversation. In his embarrassment, Roessler added that Dallow should drop in again soon, and Dallow promised he would.

He stopped at the reception desk. Barbara Schleider looked at him inquiringly, but since he didn't say anything, she finally asked whether he would once again be working at the Institute.

"It doesn't look that way," Dallow casually said, then took his coat down off the hook and put it on slowly. The secretary winced.

"Come by sometime," she said.

"Take care of yourself," answered Dallow. He left the room, and as he walked through the corridor and down the wide stairs he asked himself why he had gone to Roessler. Then he thought about Sylvia. He stopped for a moment on the stairs, turned around, and went back up. He asked the secretary for a piece of paper. On a window sill in the hallway outside the seminar rooms he wrote in large letters, I HAVE TO SLEEP WITH YOU. He went to Sylvia's classroom, knocked, and entered immediately. The students grew silent and watched him.

"I'm sorry to disturb you," apologized Dallow, "but it's very urgent. You need to sign right here, it's in your interest too, Sylvia."

He handed her the paper. She spent a long time reading the short sentence. Then she passively accepted the offered pen and said, "Yes, it does seem rather urgent."

She started to sign it, but then stopped herself and gave the paper back to Dallow.

"I'm sorry, but Roessler has to sign it first."

"He's already expressed his agreement," answered Dallow, trying to speak as formally as she.

Sylvia nodded. "That may be, but he still has to be the first to sign. Everything here has its protocol."

She was still holding the message out to Dallow. He didn't know how to respond and left without taking the paper. As he walked out he saw her smile. He tried to close the door quietly, but the latch fell shut with an annoying bang.

At the foot of the stone stairs he stopped to look at

the numerous announcements affixed to the var-
nished wood paneling. Bulletins from the Historical
Institute covered the right-hand wall. He read the
seminar rosters, but the names of the students meant
nothing to him. Back then he only taught upper-level
courses and his students had either long since left the
university or else had gone on to become assistants,
like Sylvia. The Institute's library had posted a list of
lost and stolen books. He noticed that two of the vol-
umes were in his possession, but since his name wasn't
mentioned he decided to keep them. Advertisements
offered inexpensive vacation spots to married students and students with children. He skimmed over
the seminar topics offered by the Party, they seemed
strangely familiar, he had the feeling he had already
heard all the same discussions and debates before,
back then. He went on to the offers of various Leipzig
housewives to type term papers and theses—clean
copy guaranteed at affordable prices. Then came the
colorful, gaudily framed notices of students looking
to find or trade rooms. The advertised rooms were
described in detail, with every conceivable merit
spelled out, no matter how farfetched. Dallow smiled.
Finally, he found the reading list for Sylvia's seminar.
He glanced at the titles with amusement, the same old
texts that were read, discussed, and worshiped year
in, year out. Dallow could guess which passages still
provoked debate and which sentences still evoked excitement. He took pleasure in thinking of Sylvia now

asking these ancient questions, the same beautiful Sylvia who used to beam at him with wide eyes, begging him to call on her only when both were convinced that her answer would be correct.

"God bless you, child," he said aloud to the wall covered with pieces of paper. Then he left the university.

He walked down the block, turned onto Beethovenstrasse, and looked up at the clock. Ten minutes after two. Herr Schulze will wait, he thought, and wondered whether he should keep this strange appointment. He had nothing to say to this man and there was nothing he wanted to hear from him; it would only be another stupid conversation, every bit as unnecessary as the one with Roessler. Nonetheless he continued down Beethovenstrasse, past the entrance to the Military Court and the offices of the various municipal and regional attorneys, toward the Dimitroff Museum. When he reached Harkortstrasse he noticed he was sweating. He unbuttoned the top of his coat and removed his wool scarf. The blinding winter sun and snow made him squint. The entrance to the District Court where the caller was supposed to meet him was on his right. He turned and walked toward the building. Not a soul was in sight. Two tour buses stopped on the other side of the square and deposited some tourists bound for the museum. When Dallow reached the District Court, two men suddenly appeared behind him. One of them called him by name and held out his hand. He introduced himself as Schulze and said that he was the one who had called, the other man was his colleague, Müller. He was glad that Dallow had come. Dallow just nodded without saying a word. They entered the building. Herr Schulze approached the porter's cubbyhole, spoke with the woman in attendance, and received a key. Then he asked Dallow to accompany him upstairs. Both men were wearing cheap, wrinkled worsted suits. Neither had a coat, and Dallow wondered how they had appeared so suddenly. In his surprise, he hadn't noticed exactly where they had come from.

He stopped when both men halted at one of the rooms. Herr Schulze unlocked the door, opened it, and invited Dallow to enter first.

It was a typical office with a desk, armchairs and a coffee table, the usual photographs of the leading politicians adorning the walls, a rolltop desk, and a large coat closet where files were stored. Still, something irritated Dallow, although he didn't know exactly what. He remained standing, looked around the room, and didn't sit down until he was asked. He stood up again to take off his coat and draped it over the coffee table. One of the men took it and hung it on a hook on the wall. Both men now smiled at him, which struck Dallow as silly.

"Schulze and Müller," he said doubtfully, attempting to seem reserved and distant.

Both men laughed aloud and confirmed the names were correct.

"Is it all right if I smoke?" Dallow asked and lit a cigarette before they could answer. Herr Schulze went to the wardrobe, opened it, and took out an ashtray. Dallow succeeded in catching a glimpse inside. The closet was virtually empty except for a few white cups, a typewriter, and an electric coil for boiling water. As he looked at the typewriter, the surprisingly bare shelves, and the decor which seemed sparse even for a government office, he realized immediately what it was that bothered him. The room did not contain a single human trace, no paper on the desk, no green plants, no forgotten article of clothing. There wasn't a file in sight. The office was vacant, uninhabited, unowned. It didn't even belong to these two men, thought Dallow. He had noticed that Schulze had had to think a minute where to find the ashtray.

"We're glad you came," Herr Schulze opened the conversation after everyone had sat down. "We want to help you."

Dallow felt his hands begin to shake. He was afraid his fingers would again grow stiff. Rotating red circles began to swirl before his eyes. He closed them quickly. The last time he had heard these words was twenty-one months ago, and it seemed to him they had been spoken in exactly the same obnoxiously friendly tone. The official who had interrogated him then had also leaned toward him in the same way as he assured Dallow he was only there to help.

"I don't need your help," said Dallow, his eyes still

shut. And he only opened them to ascertain whether Herr Schulze resembled his earlier interrogator. All of a sudden he was frightened by the empty, lifeless room.

"Did you lock the door?" Dallow asked the other man, who until then had only looked on in silence.

The man shook his head in surprise. "Of course not," he said. "What gave you that idea?"

Dallow was breathing through his open mouth. He wondered whether he should get up and check to see if the door really was unlocked. He now recalled that this man had stood by the door for some time after they had entered. Then he said, "May I go now?"

"Of course, anytime you like. But don't we want to talk a little first?" said Herr Schulze, puzzled.

The men's surprise calmed Dallow for the moment. He took a breath and answered: "I have no idea what we could talk about."

"I think you need help, and we can help you. That's all," answered Herr Schulze. And since Dallow only looked at him in silence, he added: "What are your plans?"

"I don't know."

"I mean what are your professional plans? Would you like to return to your Institute?"

"That's impossible. I was dismissed, and it seems they don't intend to reappoint me." He smiled as though he had just played a trump on the table.

Herr Schulze nodded. "I thought so," he said, "but I for one am not satisfied with that. I'll talk to the people in charge. If you want, you can start work again on Monday."

The offer disconcerted Dallow. "And what do I have to do in return?" he inquired suspiciously.

Now both men gave him reassuring smiles.

"Not much," replied Herr Schulze, "we help you, and you help us. That's all. We need a little information, nothing much, nothing significant, just a few tiny facts. You know, the bureaucracy always wants to know everything."

"And you're from the Municipal Council?" asked Dallow with a grin.

"No," said Herr Schulze. He reached in his jacket and removed a small I.D. card. Almost simultaneously the other man, Herr Müller, reached into his own jacket for an identical card.

"We're—" Herr Schulze began, but Dallow interrupted him to say he wasn't interested and didn't want to know. Then he turned his head toward the window to make it clear he also had no desire to see their I.D. cards.

"Work with us," said the other man, "we can help you."

"I don't need your help. Besides, I'm not going back to the Institute."

Both men seemed surprised.

"And what do you intend to do?"

"Nothing. I won't do anything," said Dallow, "I'll live off my bank account."

"And how long can you do that?" interjected Herr Müller. "One year, maybe one and a half. And then?"

"One year, that's right," answered Dallow, "I see you're well informed."

Herr Müller's face turned slightly red as he snapped back, "It was only a guess. Even we don't know everything."

"You really don't know what you'll do?" inquired Herr Schulze.

"That's right. I haven't had any time to think about it."

Herr Schulze gave a forbearing smile. "But you had the opportunity to think about it for many months."

"I've already heard that once before," said Dallow, "but it's not the case."

"You didn't have time to think about your future? What the devil did you do there?"

Dallow noticed that Herr Schulze really was amazed but that he nevertheless managed to avoid using the words "prison" or "arrest." Several times since his release he had noticed that he was the only one who pronounced the word "prison."

"I . . ." he got stuck on his answer.

Then to his own surprise he continued: "I didn't have any time. I wrote a novel while I was in prison."

"A novel?" Herr Müller repeated and grew silent.

For a few seconds the whole room was quiet. Both men observed Dallow and pondered. Dallow was amused at his inspiration. He pictured himself writing in his cell day after day, filling page after page with a scratchy fountain pen, watching the paper pile up higher and higher, the manuscript of his novel. Satisfied, he looked up and waited.

"What is your novel about? Do you intend to publish it?" asked Herr Müller. He had leaned over and seemed out of sorts.

His colleague was playing with a ballpoint pen, disinterested; then without glancing up he said, "Please, Kurt."

"Well," said Dallow, "the problem is that on the last day, the day I was released, an official came into my cell in the morning"—he paused slightly and corrected himself, bowing slightly to Herr Müller—"came into my place of custody and tore up the manuscript. My whole novel shredded, a pile of confetti."

Herr Schulze smiled and nodded, reassured.

"No?" asked Dallow.

· Herr Schulze shook his head and glanced at his colleague, who still seemed confused.

"That's too bad," said Dallow, "I have to make something up. Everybody wants to know what I did in the pen. I didn't do anything. Not even think. You can't think in there. But the whole world is convinced I had twenty-one long months to reflect upon my future. So I have to make up something, and I think the story about the novel seems like the obvious solution, for all concerned."

"It's a good story, Herr Dallow," said Herr Schulze and smiled affably, "but you forget it would mean slandering officials of the Republic. The comrades there don't tear up novels."

"Which story would you recommend?" asked Dallow. The conversation amused him now. He felt he had succeeded in distracting both men from whatever they had planned.

"Just say that one can't think while serving one's sentence. That sounds convincing enough."

"Not for everybody," objected Dallow, "it depends on your experience. But thanks for your advice. Sometimes the truth actually does sound almost persuasive."

He stood up, made a short bow, took his coat off the hook, and went to the door without a word.

"Why won't you let yourself be helped?" said Herr Schulze, as Dallow slung his coat over his arm and opened the door. "You need a good job, and you need help. And we can help you."

Dallow turned around and asked: "And why do you want to help me?"

"Because we're convinced that your conviction was a stupid mistake. It wouldn't happen today. We've made some progress since then."

He had stood up and stepped toward the door in

one motion. They stood opposite each other and looked one another in the eye.

"Oh, God," sighed Dallow, "can you give me back those two years?"

He went out and walked down the corridor to the staircase.

Behind him he heard Herr Schulze calling for him to wait. But Dallow quickened his steps, hurried down the stairs, and let the large entrance door slam shut.

The sun still seemed warm, the traffic had increased. Dallow walked up Dimitroffstrasse to his car. Once again he heard the cry: "Just wait a minute, will you?" but now it seemed unreal, like some echo inside his head, and he walked on without looking back.

That afternoon he drove into town a second time. He wanted to buy some new pants and let the saleslady advise him on the latest fashions. But in the end, against her suggestion, he chose the ones he had first selected. These pants seemed familiar to him, he explained. He decided not to buy a new winter coat, since he didn't want to spend too much money; he knew he had to have enough in the bank to be able to decide things freely, and he was afraid that rash or unnecessary expenditures might cause him to forfeit his pitiful deposit of freedom.

During the next days he organized his apartment. He went through the cabinets in his room and the kitchen, his desk, his chest of drawers. He read letters and documents and filled the small hall in his apartment with a mountain of old clothes, paper, and junk. In the evening he carried it all out back and stuffed it into the garbage bins. He gazed at the empty shelves with satisfaction; they seemed full of promise. At the sight of the free, smooth, wooden surfaces, Dallow felt encouraged.

He cooked his own dinner. Before his arrest he never found kitchen work any fun, he had left it to his girlfriends or else eaten in the student dining hall or a pub. But after two years of utterly unimaginative and poorly cooked prison fare, he had resolved to learn to cook, and devoted one hour every day to this purpose. With an open cookbook on the table he would stand in the kitchen, spice the meat, clean and finely chop the vegetables, check the progress of the pots simmering on the stove. During his first days back home he had bought a random assortment of herbs and spices; now he probed the secret of their powers. The colorful powdery spices surprised him with their varying effects and intensity of flavor. He now enjoyed preparing his food, and he recorded his experiences and discoveries in the cookbook with the same precision he had used in his research.

Every evening he drove into town and visited restaurants where people could dance. He always sat at the bar, sipped a drink and watched the women. He himself rarely danced, and when he did it was always in order to persuade his partner to spend the night with him. If the woman in question was not so inclined, or if on closer inspection he decided he didn't like her, he wouldn't ask for a second dance, just return to the bar and look around some more. After every bar visit, he slept with a different woman, but he never stayed the entire night. He didn't like waking up next to someone he didn't know; he was afraid of being disappointed in the morning, of being startled by a face without makeup. He changed bars frequently, not just to meet different women, but also to avoid running into any of his one-night acquaintances.

After a few weeks, however, he stopped visiting the bars. The unchanging routine of these evening encounters dulled his desire to the point where he felt nothing but the effort it took to approach a woman and invent some appropriate compliments. He was surprised at how quickly his lust was extinguished; after having tormented him for two years with daydreams and nightmares it now dwindled into a passionless revulsion. At first he tried to fight his growing disgust with the argument that, after all, he had some catching-up to do. But one evening he was sitting in the kitchen, all dressed to go, and simply couldn't find the strength to stand up, put on his coat, and leave. He felt nauseous and expected he would have to vomit. Half an hour later he decided not to go out that night, not to make another female friend—and his stomach settled immediately. He spent an uneventful evening at home finishing a bottle of wine and looking at old photographs.

The next evening he drove to Elke's. He rang her doorbell several times and when she didn't answer the door, he felt at once disappointment and relief. He got in his car and drove around the city for an hour. He had turned the radio up loud, and was singing along or humming to the music. He drove slowly because the falling snow made the poorly cleared streets, with their solid frozen crust of dirt, slippery and slick. His tires skidded at every turn.

As he was crossing Bayrischer Platz for the fourth

time he noticed a police car tailing him. He slowed down and observed the car in his rearview mirror. He turned onto a side street, drove past the university clinic, and again crossed Bayrischer Platz. The police car kept following him at the same speed. The street was completely deserted and quiet except for a single streetcar moving toward the fairgrounds. Suddenly the police car accelerated, passed Dallow, and a policeman signaled for him to stop. Dallow braked immediately and turned down the radio. The police drove another twenty yards before stopping and then backed up. Dallow rolled down his window and looked at them questioningly. They told him to get out. He turned off his lights and then the motor, took the key out of the ignition, and slowly rolled his window back up. Then he climbed out. One of the policemen, a short, stout man, asked to see his papers and studied them for a long time. Finally he asked what Dallow was doing there at that hour.

"I'm driving my car," said Dallow.

The policeman told him not to be smart and copied something from Dallow's papers. Next he asked for his I.D. and continued writing in his book. Dallow watched in silence.

With Dallow's papers in hand, he and his colleague then circled Dallow's car two times. They examined it thoroughly, even crouching down to look underneath. Then they returned to Dallow. The one who was holding his papers told him to get in the car and

turn on his headlights and blinkers. The policemen—
one up front, one in back—checked the lights without
the slightest change of expression. Then they approached the door and once again ordered him out.

"Citizen Dallow, your vehicle is not in operating order," said the small man.

Dallow only raised his eyebrows.

"Your right mud flap needs repair, you can't drive
with it like that."

They went behind the automobile. A corner had
broken off one of the rubber flaps behind the tires.

"But," Dallow began, then stopped when he saw the
smiling faces of the officials.

"Did you want to say something?" asked the small
man.

Dallow shook his head.

"Do you consent to a fine of twenty marks?" the policeman asked routinely and began to write out the
receipt without waiting for Dallow's reply.

"I'm giving you a deficiency ticket," continued the
policeman. "Make sure you repair it before your next
drive. By way of exception, Citizen Dallow, you may
drive home this evening. As an exception and without
any detours."

Dallow paid and took both the receipt and the
ticket without saying a word.

"Have a good drive home, Citizen Dallow," said the
small policeman in parting and walked back to the police car with his partner.

Dallow climbed in. As he pulled the door shut and heard its thin metallic clang, he realized how angry he was. He sat still in the car trying to calm down. He took deep, regular breaths as he waited for the police to drive away. But they just sat in their car and chatted. Finally Dallow turned on his lights and slowly pulled out. On the way home he checked his rearview mirror several times to see whether he was being followed. But all he saw was the empty, dimly lit street covered with snow. It was still snowing.

Friday he found a letter in his mailbox from his mother. She had heard from his sister that he had been released. She wondered why he hadn't been in touch. Then came two pages about his father and his sister's two children.

The letter made him feel ashamed. He hadn't thought of them once since his return to Leipzig. His mother had visited him during his first months in prison, but then his sister wrote that this upset the old woman so much she had to take pills, and so Dallow had asked his mother to stop coming. At the time, his mother didn't insist, since the only way they could see each other was depressing and humiliating for both of them. He corresponded with her regularly, sending longer letters than he had ever written, and he read her letters over and over, more as a distraction than out of love and devotion. Only his sister continued to visit. They had always gotten along, and it was easy for them to dismiss the indignities of prison with a few ironic remarks.

Dallow went to the post office to send his mother a telegram informing her of his plan to visit the coming Sunday. He had to wait in line a long time and was annoyed he hadn't sent the telegram by phone. Nonetheless he waited with the others until he was finally able to pass his completed form to the woman behind the counter.

On the way home he wondered why he hadn't contacted his family. He had nothing to do. He enjoyed frittering away his time without obligations, without being bossed around. In his fleeting relations with women, he had been careful always to leave without discussing future meetings or even hinting at them. He was astounded how easily this came to him. At first he felt he had to resort to excuses and white lies to avoid the slightest commitment, no matter how trivial. But when it came time to leave, when the conversation faltered and man and woman sat facing one another without making a move, when there was nothing more to say than some vague remark about getting together sometime, when every additional comment only further revealed what was better left concealed, when the act of putting on his coat seemed to command his entire attention while the woman looked on from where she lay in bed or from where she stood by the door to let him out—Dallow soon noticed that in these moments of leaving, he needed only to be silent in order to be understood. It was easy to leave, he discovered, if you just didn't say anything. Words complicate even the simplest subject and in the end don't clarify anything. He was pleased to have found such a pleasant and convenient solution to the problem, or, actually, a way of avoiding it altogether.

By taking each day as it came he thus managed to steer clear of all appointments, dates, and commitments. Nor had he contacted any friends or acquaintances—except for a very few, and these mostly by chance. He wanted to begin slowly and on his own, he needed time. He realized he had to learn to live outside his cell. The littlest things had to be relearned, since words and gestures meant something different outside prison than they did inside. His cell, as he now discovered, had been a familiar environment, a home, safe and secure, and no matter how ardently he had desired and longed for it, freedom had become alien and strange.

He realized he was now constructing another cell for himself, solitary and isolated, and that he was anxiously checking that the door stayed locked. He now sensed why he hadn't contacted his friends. He didn't want to receive visitors, he didn't need anywhere to go. He feared the first conversations, those awkward, considerately phrased questions about his time in prison, his own invariable replies, the excuses he used to avoid chronicling all the tiresome details of the past two years. People wanted to show their sympathy, and yet that was precisely what kept sending him back to prison, back to the time he wanted to forget quickly and completely. But they kept forcing him to recollect it, to behold it, in order to describe and ultimately color events so that his life in prison seemed wilder, more picturesque and more frightening than it had really been. He was glad to escape these conversations, but at the same time he was surprised that not a single one of his friends had looked him up. Of course it was up to him to get in touch, to get back in touch, but still he had the feeling his friends were avoiding him. Harry, Roessler, Sylvia had all seen him—word must have gotten around that he was out of prison. But everyone left him alone. He wasn't really upset, but he did find it puzzling. Certainly some friends, particularly the older ones, considered him branded for life. For them prison was dishonorable, no matter what the cause of arrest. That was all right, he had learned to cope with that. He knew that one way or another, these two years would accompany him to his death. He would always be the man who had spent two years in jail; neither he nor the others would ever forget it. It's like a harelip, he told himself, you just have to learn to live with it. Maybe the others realized this, and so they kept away out of sympathy, the same sympathy that would otherwise oblige them to ask about his time of shame. It was apparently unpleasant for everyone. He didn't want to talk about it and his friends didn't want to hear about it. And since they nonetheless felt obliged to inquire and express their compassion, and since that only placed a burden on all parties, they preferred to avoid him altogether. Sympathy's a wonderful thing, he thought, and smiled with satisfaction. He had his peace, at least for now.

Just as he had unlocked the door to go inside the house he saw Stämmler walking up the street. He waited. Stämmler didn't notice him until Dallow stepped right in front of him. Stämmler was startled at first but then greeted Dallow cordially. He lived in the next building, on the top floor. He and his wife had occasionally visited Dallow or invited him over—maybe two or three times a year. Stämmler was an engineer who worked as a manager for a Leipzig machine factory where he was responsible for the export of printing equipment. Dallow appreciated his intelligence and wit and liked to listen to Stämmler's wild stories about the factory and his various business dealings.

Dallow was amused to notice that Stämmler seemed embarrassed and had even turned a little red. He listened quietly as his neighbor assured him that he had no idea Dallow was already back. He, Stämmler, would like to get together one of these evenings. Stämmler also avoided the word prison.

Then both were silent. A young woman came toward them, pulling a child in a sled. The men stepped aside to let her pass. The mother stooped slightly as she dragged the heavy sled across the sidewalk from which most of the snow had been swept. The child pointed a small red plastic machine gun at the two men and imitated the clatter of gunfire. "Stop that, Silvio," said the mother without turning around.

Both men glanced back at the child, enveloped in woolen blankets, who grimaced as he continued to fire away, spraying them with imaginary bullets.

Dallow turned to Stämmler and asked about his wife.

"There's no way you could know," Stämmler replied, "we had another child."

Dallow congratulated him.

"But it's another boy," parried Stämmler, "and this time Doris was absolutely sure it was going to be a girl."

"How old is the little one?"

"A little over a year. His name is Alexander." He added melancholically: "It was supposed to be Susanne. But now we're giving up."

He passed his mesh shopping bag from one hand to the other and blew on his fingers which were red from the cold. Then he stomped his feet and smiled at Dallow who was standing there at a complete loss. "I have to go," Stämmler said at last, "Doris is waiting. Drop by sometime. You know you're always welcome. And we're home almost every night, with the children."

They said goodbye. As he walked the few yards to his house, Stämmler turned around twice and waved to Dallow who was still standing at his door.

That evening for the first time Dallow felt the despair and unsettling void of loneliness. He wandered from room to room and rummaged through the scant contents of his desk. He caught himself sitting on one of the kitchen stools, tapping on the wall and expecting an answering knock. In prison, he had never felt lonely. There he had had unusual neighbors who aroused his curiosity, people he had never come across before, whose behavior and opinions took him utterly by surprise. They remained alien to him, sometimes disconcertingly so. Some he avoided out of fear, others because they repelled or disgusted him. But there were also always a few to talk to or simply listen to for hours on end. Moreover there were the short but regular encounters with his official custodians whom he despised and scorned without exception and between whom he was unwilling to make any distinctions. He had soon given up all verbal conflict with them; such altercations were senseless and produced no practical result. But even his unspoken scorn lent him strength and hope, and the solidarity with his cellmates afforded him peace and security—although this was quite ridiculous since the solidarity stemmed from circumstance alone and would never have withstood the slightest, most banal argument.

He examined his red knuckles and overcame the

mindless desire to keep drumming on the kitchen wall. He was amazed how inept and ill-prepared he was for freedom. He hadn't thought he would have to do so much adapting; he was convinced that after his release he would just go on living the way he had in the years preceding his arrest, that he would return to familiar circumstances and, guided by habit, would once again allow the gentle, lazy flow of everyday life to carry him along. He was surprised that these earlier years, his former life, had become unattainable, impossible to resume. Naturally he kept telling himself that this was his chance for a completely new beginning, that rare stroke of fortune that permitted a truly fresh start, he had only to avail himself of the opportunity. But he was gripped by anxieties he could barely understand, possessed by an insecurity that sent him spinning around in circles—and he had great difficulty suppressing the desire to sit down at the piano and play one of the few sonatas he knew by heart.

Around midnight, when he collapsed into bed after having unintentionally emptied a bottle of brandy, the only clear thought to emerge from his brooding and his conversations with himself was the decision to give his apartment a thorough cleaning the next morning.

He woke up late and with a headache that even a cold shower could not fix. The cleaning kept him busy through the evening. He was amazed at the apparently inexhaustible amounts of dirt on the floor and furniture of his apartment. The work strained him, since he performed it reluctantly, all the while mourning the wasted time. He was so fatigued he lost his appetite, and all he could do in the evening was sit in front of the television with a cup of coffee. He heard the anchorwoman and stared at the pictures without really taking them in. When he noticed he was beginning to snooze he stood up, turned the television off, and went to bed. At two in the morning he woke up— he thought he had heard the telephone ring. He stayed in bed, listening, but everything was quiet. He lay awake for a long time afterward, continuing his self-analysis, and didn't fall back asleep until he had reset his alarm.

By eight o'clock he was on the autobahn. He drove at a modest speed and accelerated evenly. He was afraid his car might have suffered from the long layoff and wouldn't be fit for a serious trip, but the engine ran smoothly and without any unusual noises. He, in return, was so pleased that he spoke tenderly to his automobile throughout the entire trip, cautioning it to be careful and giving it all the encouragement he could. He knew he was being silly, and whenever drivers in passing cars looked his way they were bound to think him either mentally disturbed or uncommonly excited. Dallow would then wave politely and shout something inaudible through closed windows to his bewildered observers.

At midday he arrived at his parents' village, the tiny community where he had spent his entire childhood. For fourteen years he had ventured beyond this village only as far as his rickety child's bicycle would take him. Although he seldom thought about the village, it often appeared as the setting of his dreams, as if every actual event of his waking life, every phantasm of the night's unreal reality—of which he was scarcely conscious and which he could barely reconstruct the next morning—had been determined by things he had experienced in this place. And so he remained tied to the village in an unconscious and completely incomprehensible manner.

This was where it had all begun, the yearnings and unpronounceable desires that carried him off time and again, out of his small nest into lost times and rich and happier worlds, borne on the wings of daydreams inspired by books borrowed from the community library. Until one day they literally led him out of the village and into another life. Driving back to the village for the first time since his release, he sensed how his life kept all gain and loss in balance, that up to now and to the end of his days he would be refereeing a zero sum game.

Dallow's parents lived in the middle of the village, in a house opposite the small fork in the street that enclosed the former school and its tiny garden. In the absence of a more suitable village square, this island served as a public meeting place on holidays.

Dallow parked his car in front of the courtyard gate. He glanced at the stone stairs and the concrete landing bordered by two small cast-iron benches and, further back, the double entrance doors. He refrained from going up. There hadn't been more than twenty days that these doors had been used since the house was built, and then only to celebrate a wedding or host a funeral reception. They remained closed even on birthdays, and friends from the village would enter the house as they always did, by crossing the courtyard.

When Dallow entered the courtyard and cast his eyes over the barn and stall, everything seemed unchanged. But then he noticed the roof, hopelessly in need of repair, the broken door to the stall, the decrepit farm tools piling up in a corner of the yard. Taken aback, he tried to calculate his father's age. He crossed the small porch that connected the back of the house with the courtyard. In the kitchen he greeted and embraced his mother. She kept stroking his hands and asking him one question after another without waiting for his replies. Then she called his father and urged the men to sit on the porch. She brought beer and brandy and cigarettes and ran back into the kitchen to fix dinner. Again and again she would interrupt her work to briefly join the men on the porch, ask a question, and then disappear before her son could answer.

Dallow sat next to his father on the corner bench without saying a word. They clinked their small glasses together and stole glances at one another. Dallow had the impression that his father had aged more quickly during the last two years. When he first came in he had noticed that his father was dragging his right leg, but since he apparently wanted to hide the problem, Dallow refrained from asking and waited for his father to bring up the subject.

"I didn't visit you," the old farmer finally began, "because I . . ."

He hesitated, and his son nodded and said, "I understand, Father, it was better that way. Besides, I know the farm doesn't let you get away."

The old man crinkled his eyes together and looked out over his farmyard. He shook his head slowly and replied: "No, Peter, it wasn't the farm. I didn't visit you because I couldn't bring myself to do it."

Dallow noticed how his father's hands were shaking and wanted to place his own hand on top of them to keep them still. But he only turned his head and looked out over the farmyard. All he noticed was how the stalls and the barn had deteriorated. He looked at the farm his father had abandoned.

"It was better that way," he said, "it wasn't a place for visiting."

The farmer again shook his head, dissatisfied. "No," he said stubbornly, "it wasn't that. I didn't go because it was impossible for me to visit my son in prison."

Dallow looked at his father and countered with unintended sharpness: "There wasn't anything for me to be ashamed of. Nothing whatsoever."

"But it was prison," his father persisted stubbornly.

It pained Dallow to have to defend himself again only to be condemned again. "Oh, Father," he sighed, "prison is just another place to kill time."

"I see it differently, and I think that the people here where you grew up also see it differently."

"I'm sure of that. People here think differently about a lot of things. I'll just have to cope with that."

A cow lowed, and two others lowed in reply.

"That's not the way I brought you up," said Dallow's father, who then finished his beer and banged the glass on the table.

"It wasn't my wish to sit in prison for two years. But the only thing I might be guilty of is that I can play the piano a little. And you and Mother are more responsible for that than I am, since you sent me into town every week for four years straight, you paid for a music teacher, and you put a piano in the living room for me. If I landed in jail after all that effort and devotion it's not my fault. You'll remember it wasn't easy for me to learn to play. And if I had had any notion of how much it was going to cost in the long run, believe me, I would have resisted you more stubbornly."

His father looked at him dully and without understanding. And before the old man could find the words to formulate the question, his son answered: "Yes, Father, the truth is that ridiculous. Any madeup story would be easier to believe."

"You forget that you showed your mother the verdict in writing. I read that paper over and over. There's nothing about a piano in it."

"That only shows that the truth was so pitiful that not even the judge could bring himself to say it."

The two men looked each other in the eye so unflinchingly, so determined, that every turning away, every blink seemed a judgment, and Dallow understood that his visit had not ended his father's despair, that his imprisonment remained a shameful vexation, and that he would have to accept this without resistance, without defending himself, and without satisfying his sense of justice, his sense of honor. And then Dallow understood that he would have to abandon his intention and explain the entire tedious and banal story in order to give himself a chance to find his peace.

He grabbed his glass, swallowed his reluctance along with the brandy, and described that Tuesday when he had been sitting in his office with Roessler when there was a knock at the door. Three students entered: one he knew from his seminars, the others he recognized from performances of the student cabaret. He greeted them amiably, without realizing what they really were, the harbingers of his ill fortune, the three black ravens who instead of coming one by one came all at once to crow their bleak prognostication. The students asked him to step in and save their opening performance, which had been announced for the following evening. Their piano player had been taken to the university clinic that morning with a hernia, and in order to save their show they had to find a new pianist, someone who supported what they were doing and was willing to learn their program in the few hours that remained.

"Actually," said Dallow, "the students were all terrible dilettantes, and looking for a musician to match. That's why they came to me."

He had told them that as far as he was concerned it sounded like an invitation to close his eyes and leap into an abyss. He declined. But the students were desperate and wouldn't give up. They kept explaining their situation, they pleaded and begged and promised he would only have to cover for two performances, the third was scheduled for a week later and by that time either the original pianist, who had composed the songs, would be out of the hospital or else they would have found another substitute. They mentioned that the performance had been approved by the university administration, so there wasn't the slightest danger of a ban or other trouble, in case that was the cause of Dallow's hesitation. At that, Dallow simply laughed out loud and replied, "The problem is with my digestion. Officially approved jokes make me nauseous."

But then he took the score and promised to look it over. He spent two hours at home practicing, and it turned out that the music was easier than antici-pated—the songs were mostly old hits and standards whose texts had been slightly rewritten. The students called him at seven o'clock, as arranged. He promised to come to their rehearsal. All he requested for the performance was an overlarge pair of sunglasses. He wasn't afraid that he might be recognized, he ex-plained, but that he would blind the audience with his face glowing with shame.

The last and, for Dallow, the only rehearsal was a carnival of gaffes, as he put it. After every song, the given performer would apologize and Dallow would listen to the excuses sternly and in silence. It was agreed that he would play fortissimo to keep the stu-dents on track.

"I only wish," Dallow said to his father, "I had played so loud on opening night that no one in the audience would have understood a single word."

The performance received friendly applause. Of course the students themselves had the most fun, es-pecially at the cast party, which went on for four hours, in which they recalled all their misspoken lines and technical mishaps.

At eight o'clock the next morning Dallow was awakened by the doorbell. Two uniformed officials presented him with a warrant for his arrest and took him to be interrogated.

"I spent the first two days in a cell, Father, without the slightest clue what I was doing there. I was sure it had to be a mistake," he said forcibly.

From the first cell, where he spent seven weeks, he could look out and see the prison yard, a wall, and the windows of his Institute, which was located in the second story of a building the District Court had leased to the university just after the war for an indefinite time. He often stared at those windows, and occasionally he could make out colleagues and students, but the distance was so great he was never certain whether they were really there or whether he was just succumbing to an illusion. Since he had never before seen the windows that overlooked the jail from the outside, he remained uncertain to his very last day in that cell whether they really were the people he took them to be.

The indictment charged him with insulting leaders of the state. Dallow asked the defense lawyer assigned to him by the court to explain the charge. The lawyer showed him the texts to the songs that formed the basis of the accusation; Dallow was seeing them for the first time in his cell, since he hadn't been able to pay any attention to them during the rehearsal and the performance. He discovered that the lyrics to a tango from the twenties had been slightly altered to poke fun at the aging head of state—though only half-heartedly, and very blandly, Dallow thought.

"The lyrics are awful," said Dallow after he had looked them over.

His counsel nodded and replied happily: "Tell that to the court."

"There's no wit," continued Dallow, "no bite, no punch."

Herr Kiewer, his counsel, looked at him blankly. Then he nodded solemnly and said in a resigned voice, "I suggest you refrain from sharing your opin-ion of the text with the judge. During the hearing it will be best to limit our answers to a simple yes or no."

Dallow agreed. Nevertheless he was surprised that this was all his lawyer had to say concerning his court-room strategy. And when Herr Kiewer wanted to end his first and only visit to the jail cell after only eight minutes, Dallow asked anxiously whether that was all he needed to know.

Kiewer, a corpulent fifty-year-old man, had already stood up and was reaching for his overcoat. In the open cell door he turned again to Dallow, spread his arms in a habitual gesture, so that the black briefcase in his right hand swung high over the floor, and stated, "If you have any other questions, please feel free. My time is your time, I am at your disposal. But don't forget I'm defending your entire group. And besides that, I have other cases as well."

Dallow was at a loss. He had no further questions and excused himself: "I have no experience with this. I've never been in jail before."

Kiewer seemed to understand. "I wouldn't worry about it," he said as he nodded thankfully to the official waiting to close the door, "your case doesn't look all that bad."

Dallow looked at his father and repeated: " 'Your case doesn't look all that bad'—those were his exact words. My God, Father, how long would I have been there if it had looked bad?"

The hearing took place three weeks later. Dallow declared his innocence, which he supported by explaining that he hadn't seen the text to the song in question until he was in his jail cell. The judge found this doubtful, considering that Dallow had rehearsed the same song with the group of students.

Dallow repeated what he had told his counsel in the cell: "I received the music twenty-four hours before the performance. I practiced it for two hours by myself. In the remaining time and even during the performance I spent all of my energy trying to convey to the students some faint notion of the musical phenomenon known as rhythm. How was I supposed to pay any attention to the lyrics? In fact, I kept thinking my time would be better spent teaching color theory in a school for the blind."

The judge answered with essentially the same words his lawyer had used three weeks earlier in the cell when Dallow had told him the same thing: "That would have been better for all concerned."

Because no one took responsibility for the text—the students insisted it had originated spontaneously during a rehearsal—all defendants received the same sentence: twenty-one months including detention pending investigation. Like all the other defendants, Dallow had the opportunity to comment on the sentence once it was pronounced; he simply turned to the judge and stated: "I am amazed you didn't sentence me to twenty-one years. After all, for you it's just a different word."

The judge rebuked him earnestly for this remark, but not without a satisfied smile.

Dallow played with his empty beer glass and waited for his father to react to his report. The old farmer looked down at his hands helplessly, his breathing was audible but he didn't say a single word. So Dallow completed his tale: "I had to say that to the judge, Father. He wasn't going to lose a single minute of sleep on my account. I owed myself at least that much."

"Dinner's on the table, come and eat," said his mother. She was leaning on the door frame, and a quiet trembling in her voice revealed that she had been listening to her son.

"Twenty-one months," said the old man, and that was all he could say after having absorbed his son's report and given it some consideration.

"Just forget the whole thing," Dallow said, holding his father's arm, "I barely remember it myself."

He stood up and followed his mother into the living room.

After dinner they returned to the porch. His mother talked about Gerda, Dallow's sister, who lived in the district capital with her husband and children. Then she said that Marion had finally had a child and that she had been very proud and had stopped by to show off the baby. Marion was Dallow's former wife. They had married at nineteen and divorced a year later. Now she lived in a neighboring village; Dallow hadn't seen her since the divorce. He listened to his mother in silence, and even when she interrupted herself and looked at him quizzically, he didn't react.

His mother changed the subject after a short pause and talked about her husband's disability; he had come back from the front with a bad leg.

"It didn't bother him for twenty-five years, but now it's making itself felt again," she said. "You know Father never complains, and he won't go to any doctor. But when he dreams he screams so loud he wakes me up."

"You're wrong, Margarete," the farmer butted in, "I don't scream, and I don't dream. I just talk to myself out loud because I know that then you'll have to listen to me without constantly interrupting."

"Don't be silly." Then to her son: "Just look how he walks. Or just look at the farm and you'll know all there is to know."

Dallow's father snarled back: "What do you expect? Should I put a new roof on the barn? For whom? I might as well sell everything off and we could move to the city. In one of those apartments where you don't have to do anything but turn a faucet and push some button."

Dallow didn't say anything. He knew how frustrated his father was that none of the children wanted to take over the farm. But he himself was too far removed from it all, he didn't belong anymore, he hadn't felt at home here for a long time, he couldn't live here anymore.

An hour later he accompanied his mother into the cowshed to feed the animals. He had put on his father's rubber boots and was pitching straw and hay down from the loft. Then he cut up the stale bread and patiently answered his mother's many little questions. He had to assure her several times that he was doing well and only once he didn't know how to respond—when she said abruptly, "The garden has to be turned over again. I don't know what to do. Father can't manage anymore."

That evening he went to the train station and called

his sister from the stationmaster's office. They agreed to meet at her place the next evening.

The stationmaster was sitting at his desk. He had dropped his pen and was leaning back in his chair so he could better listen to the conversation. He would nod in agreement whenever one of Dallow's remarks seemed appropriate.

After Dallow finished, they waited for the operator to call back and say how much the conversation cost. The stationmaster invited him to sit down but Dallow declined and examined the rail network chart posted on the wall behind the three public telephones. He liked the idea of a map that portrayed the country solely in terms of the needs and interests of the railway company. Only those cities and connecting stations that had significance for the railroad were depicted. Where no tracks existed, the map showed patches of white, no-man's-land, wilderness.

Dallow made a mental draft of his own map. This ridiculously small village would be its central point, the capital. Leipzig, where he had studied and taught, would appear considerably smaller but still impossible to overlook. The city where he had been imprisoned would be allotted the same significance, or actually just the prison itself since he never got to know the city. Then there would be a few small resort towns on the Baltic, the Harz Mountains, the Masurian lake district, and Georgia could be seen, as well as a few tiny dots representing Cracow, Prague, Budapest, and Moscow. The next years would add a few cities and landscapes, but the palm of his hand would still suffice for his personal world atlas. After all, I'm not a railway company, he told himself.

Immersed in these thoughts, Dallow absentmindedly answered the stationmaster's questions. He realized that the stationmaster was asking him for the third time where he had been the past couple of years, why he hadn't been out to see his parents.

"You're well informed," he said. "For the past two years I've been eating off a tin plate and shitting in a bucket in my cell."

"The official smiled apologetically. "People talk a lot around here," he said defensively, "I don't pay it any mind. Usually half of it isn't true anyway."

One of the telephones rang. The man picked up the receiver and answered. Then he jotted something down on a piece of paper lying on the desk in front him, spoke a few numbers and the time into the receiver, and hung up. He went to the switchboard in the back of the room, adjusted two levers, and looked right and left through the small window facing the tracks, out into the night. Then he sat back down at the desk. Two whittling knives and a pile of wood shavings lay amidst the papers; several small wood figures, some of them painted, adorned the windowsill.

"Do you mind if I ask," the man began once again, "why you . . ." He didn't finish his question.

Dallow looked at him uncertainly. "That's a difficult question," he said.

It's pointless to try to explain it to you, he thought, the story is too unbelievable, even if I tell it in its entirety every time.

"I don't know whether you can understand this, but the only reason I landed in prison for two years was because that's what the judge ruled."

The man reached for one of his knives. Then he smiled, looked at Dallow, and said, "I can understand. I know how to read between the lines."

He picked up one of the figurines and started to shave it timidly. "In my work," he continued, "you're always standing with one leg in the pen. One missed signal and off you go."

Dallow nodded without being terribly convinced, partly because he had heard too many stories like that, partly because he was again studying the map.

The telephone rang. The stationmaster picked up the receiver and listened without saying a word. "Ninety pfennigs," he told Dallow as he hung up.

Dallow paid and said goodbye.

Next morning he rose early to help his mother feed the animals and milk the two cows. Then they sat for a long time at the breakfast table on the porch. His parents talked about working in the cooperative; as he listened to them he began to envy their constant satisfaction.

"And what about your work, Peter?" asked his mother.

Dallow had been fearing this question all weekend but it still took him completely by surprise. He smiled at her and considered what to say. He knew it was out of the question for him to tell his parents that he hadn't worked since the day he was released and that, moreover, he intended to keep it that way as long as his money lasted. He couldn't explain to them what it meant for him to escape even the slightest constraint, why he had to avoid any and all permanent situations. He couldn't say that he simply didn't want to work anymore. For them, that would be even more difficult to swallow than the news of his arrest had been.

"There are still a few problems that have to be worked out," he said very slowly. "When I was arrested they dismissed me, and that's still my official status."

His parents didn't say a thing, and for a moment Dallow once again became the little schoolboy forced to explain some silly incident as they listened in punishing silence.

"I'm constantly meeting with people from the Institute," he lied to reassure them, "with all types of people. My guess is that in the next few days . . ."

His father broke in. "You mean you haven't been working for three weeks?"

"It's complicated, Father, there are problems with

the labor laws. This kind of thing takes time, but it's basically just a bureaucratic problem. And besides, a few good friends who have the necessary connections are helping me."

He began to sweat. Some good friends, he thought: the only people who want to help me are Herr Schulze and Herr Müller. How could he possibly be describing them to his parents as his friends, his good friends.

His father cleared his throat, then said very calmly and firmly: "Come back. Take over the farm. You can work in the cooperative or else in town, it'll work out somehow. But take over the farm. I can't manage anymore. Everything's falling apart."

"I'm not a farmer," answered Dallow in torment.

The old man shook his head. "That will all work itself out. You have work here. You have a farm here. And half the house as well. And if you don't want to live here we'll build an addition. Or else we'll buy the empty wing from the cooperative."

Dallow shook his head firmly. He closed his eyes and said, "It's too late, Father. I don't belong here anymore."

The old farmer looked at his wife.

"It's all right," she said, "let him be. He wouldn't be happy here."

"But the farm," the old man started up again, but he stopped short when he met his wife's gaze.

They didn't speak about it anymore. But Dallow noticed that his father kept eyeing him, brooding, whenever he thought his son wasn't watching.

Late in the afternoon he took his leave and drove out to his sister's. His mother gave him a shopping bag containing jars of homemade sausage and some eggs. As he hugged his parents goodbye his father only looked at him in silence. He stared helplessly, a silent plea. But his son had no reply.

It was getting dark when Dallow reached the district capital where his sister lived. Since he had rarely visited her he had to ask some passersby for directions.

His brother-in-law, Sebastian, opened the door and let him in. They looked each other over without saying a word.

"It's nice you're here," Sebastian finally broke the silence and embraced him. "Gerda will be happy to see you."

Sebastian helped Dallow out of his coat and showed him into the living room.

"Have a seat," he said, and without asking filled two glasses with cognac.

Dallow asked about his sister and when he heard she was putting the two daughters to bed he confessed he had forgotten to bring them a present.

"Exactly as I expected," his brother-in-law said sympathetically. "You never were interested in girls that young." And when Dallow insisted on seeing his nieces, Sebastian handed him a bar of chocolate big enough to give to both.

When he entered the children's room his sister cried out, ran to him and hugged him. He tried to calm her down and gently pushed her away, but she held on to him tightly with both arms, sobbed loudly and kissed him over and over. The two girls sat up in their beds and watched their mother and this unknown man with amazement and with fear.

Dallow ran his hand over his sister's hair and smiled reassuringly at the two children.

"I suggest," he said, "you let me catch my breath and then I'll say hello to your children."

But she no sooner let him out of her arms than she grabbed his hands and lay her head on his chest. Kissing her hair, Dallow carefully extracted himself from her grip. He went over to the girls, sat down on one of the beds and spoke to them. They didn't remember him; they remained solemn and subdued and didn't react to anything he said. When he offered them the chocolate they neither smiled nor accepted the gift. He had to leave it at the edge of the bed.

"They're tired," his sister explained, "we were running around Berlin all day."

Dallow kissed the girls and left the room. He sat down in the living room while his sister cooked some supper for him. Then they all sat down together for a long time and drank a lot. They talked about their parents, about their own childhood and about Dallow's nieces, and it wasn't until Dallow got up to go to bed that his sister said, "I have the feeling, Peter, there's something else you should tell us."

Dallow sighed. "Don't forget," he said shaking his head, "I've already had to tell this story quite a few times. And before telling it the first time I had to live it. And even that bored me to tears."

"Sit back down," said his sister, "because you still have to tell it to me."

"That's like asking me to relive it," Dallow said dismally and began to tell the story. He took pains to report everything quickly and objectively, but his sister's questions made him stop several times and fill in the details.

"And what song was it?" asked his brother-in-law after he had finished.

"It was an old tango, 'Adiós, muchachos.' "

"I know it. 'Adiós muchachos, compañeros de mi vida,' " exclaimed Sebastian gleefully and hummed the melody.

Dallow winced and nodded.

"A tango," said Sebastian, satisfied, "I should have guessed as much. Anyway, you don't play tangos on a piano. You need a bandonion. Maybe that was what annoyed your judge so much."

Dallow nodded his head. "At least then I'd know

why I spent two years in prison. But even if that was his reason, it would still be the most expensive tango ever."

"Not so," said his brother-in-law, as he stood up to refill their glasses. Holding the bottle in his hand, he explained: "You can read statistics showing that every one of those sad old tangos has more suicides on its conscience than this country has whores who were once virgins."

"We should let you get to bed," said Dallow's sister, attempting to wrest the bottle from her husband.

"When I drove the ambulance. . ."

Dallow laughed aloud. "Is he still talking about that?" he asked his sister. "Is he still going on about his glorious ambulance?"

"Naturally," she said, "they must have been the happiest years of his life."

Her husband protested. "It was hard work. We were fined if we went too fast, and if we went too slow and the patient died we also had to pay. We constantly had one leg in the pen."

Dallow nodded. "I've already heard that expression once," he said. "The whole country seems to be standing with one leg in the pen. Except for the prisoners and their wardens."

"An unfortunate image," conceded Sebastian. "All I wanted to say was that we were really afraid of those damned tangos. I suggested to the dispatcher that we

drive slowly through the city every Sunday afternoon
and wherever we heard those sad old tangos being
played too loudly we should break down the door and
maybe manage to cut somebody down from the ceiling before he became a corpse. But they didn't listen:
our supervisor insisted we'd only be interrupting the
creation of some new human being."

His wife giggled.

"During a tango?" asked Dallow incredulously.
"Impossible. A tango isn't suited for that at all. No,
no, not a tango. Bach is much better, the *Brandenburg
Concerti,* and Ravel's *Bolero.* Café music, also accept-
able, and most of Mozart. But you can't fuck to a
tango. A tango inhibits you, and the rhythm's all
wrong. Didn't you learn anything at the university?
What did they teach you?"

"Stop it," demanded Gerda, "I feel like I'm sitting
with a couple of schoolboys."

Dallow kissed the tips of her fingers in fun.

"Everything all right?" he asked. She nodded. Later
they talked about their parents.

"They've grown old," said Dallow, and all nodded in
silence.

His brother-in-law told Dallow how he had tried to
get them to move into town with them. He had even
found them a buyer.

"But they didn't want to," he said, "and I can understand them."

"Sure," said Dallow, "but that doesn't help anybody. They want one of us to take over the farm. We could draw straws to decide. The short straw takes over and becomes a farmer."

"Why should it be the loser?" asked Sebastian. "Why shouldn't the winner get the farm?"

Dallow looked at him in surprise and thought for a moment.

The next morning he ate breakfast with the family and they all left the house together. They said goodbye at his car and he drove back to Leipzig. On the way home he thought about his parents and told himself that he should find some kind of work if only to reassure them. A job, he said to himself, any old job. He considered the possibilities at hand and rejected them all. And as the distance from his parent's village grew, his oppressive feeling of obligation to them lessened. By the time he left the autobahn the idea of finding work for the sake of his parents seemed nothing short of absurd. He felt relieved as he drove into the city.

That evening he washed his clothes and sewed buttons on his shirts. As he sat in front of the television, his old yellow wooden sewing box and a stack of shirts on the table beside him, he tried to feel amused by the picture he presented. But he was unsuccessful. A frightful image kept intruding, of old age, and a lonely man living out his years. He hastily finished the work he had begun, threw the clothes on the armchair, got up, pulled on his overcoat, and quickly left the apartment. He waited until he was outside before adjusting his scarf and buttoning his coat, his fingers twitching nervously. He passed through the dimly lit streets and tried hard to shake the panicky fright that had taken possession of him so suddenly. He tried to chase away his worries, but he couldn't rely on logic to dispel the haunting vision, precisely because he found it so inexplicable. He stopped twice to light a cigarette in the doorway of some apartment building, but both times it fell out of his numb fingers onto the dirty street. He paused in front of the neighborhood movie theater. The inside doors were closed for a late showing. Music and unintelligible words escaped through the small windows of the projection room into the lobby. The showcases were still lit, Dallow studied the stills from the movies attentively. He made an effort to calm down and concentrate on the pictures. He tried to judge the films by the photos and decide whether he might be interested in seeing them. He looked at well-dressed men in apparently heated conversations and half-dressed women in apparently dangerous situations. Dallow decided he couldn't tell anything from the photos and went on to read the blurbs on the posters. Just then the lights in the showcases went out, a few seconds later the neon sign over the moviehouse was also extinguished, and the bluish, radiant word C I N E M A sank into the black, nearly invisible façade. He focused on that word, he reflected on it, he liked it.

He stopped in front of a pub next to the private garden plots. The little cabins were entirely dark. The owners were still in the city in their heated apartments. Dallow was freezing, and although it wasn't his kind of place, he went inside.

A warm beery mist hit him as soon as he opened the inside door. All the tables were taken, and for a few seconds all conversation ceased and the faces turned to Dallow. Just like a country tavern, he thought. From an earlier visit he remembered the customary ritual of greeting and walked slowly toward the back, lightly rapping his knuckles on the tables. The seated men returned the greeting without speaking by letting the tips of their fingers fall on the scrubbed wooden surface of the tables.

At one table in front of the door to the toilet a woman was sitting with a man. Dallow pointed to a chair and asked them if it was free. The young woman nodded and Dallow sat down. When he pulled a cigarette out of a pack the woman reached for her matches, lit one, and held it out for him. Dallow was surprised, thanked her, and took the burning match from her fingers to light his cigarette.

"Philosopher," said the man suddenly.

Dallow perked up and tried to look the man over as

casually as possible. He was in his mid-fifties, his face was very ruddy and the skin on his hands was cracked. Tanned by the elements, Dallow noted to himself with irony and looked around the room.

In the same calm voice the man repeated, "Philosopher."

Dallow had assumed the man was talking to the young woman, but now he understood that he was being addressed and responded tentatively: "I don't understand."

"He's asking if you're a philosopher," explained the woman.

Dallow glanced at the glowing end of his cigarette. A madhouse, he thought. He looked at the man and answered, "No." And added: "I just want to drink a beer."

He waited impatiently for the waiter. The man and woman were also silent, but Dallow no longer had the impression that they had broken off their conversation on his account. He guessed they had been sitting here the entire evening, drinking their beer in silence. Married, no doubt, he thought with pleasure.

When the waiter appeared the woman ordered before Dallow could open his mouth: "The gentleman would like a beer, please." And she pointed at Dallow.

The waiter looked at him, Dallow confirmed the order by nodding his head. "And a clear whiskey. Rye."

The waiter brought the beer and the rye whiskey,

placed both on a large round cardboard coaster and made some marks with his pencil. Dallow downed the whiskey and took a swallow of beer.

"What do you think about the world?" the man asked.

Dallow put down his beer glass and said uncertainly, "Are you asking me?"

The man nodded.

"Well," said Dallow. Then he cleared his throat and tried to get out of it by saying, "That's a big question, chief, too big for tonight."

"It's a good question," said the man disapprovingly.

The woman next to him stared at Dallow openmouthed and waited for his answer.

Two people from the loony bin who've been sitting around, just waiting for a sucker like me, Dallow thought and resolved to pay and leave at once.

"So what do you think?" the man repeated.

Dallow drew his eyes together slightly and said quickly and without further reflection, "A cinema. The world is a cinema."

The woman now turned her eyes on the man, quizzically. Dallow's answer seemed to surprise him.

"Philosophically grounded," he decided after a long pause.

Dallow protested. "No, no, I don't mean it philosophically. You can take it physically or biologically or chemically or however you want, just not philosophically. It's a very simple truth, no philosophy is needed. When the big lamp is turned off there won't be anything left. All existence is bound to the light and so it really doesn't exist. It's just a light show, an optical phenomenon like the cinema. Or water dancing in a fountain. And what are light shows and electric fountains? Sheer follies, time-killers, made of nothing. You flick a switch and what's left? A dark screen and a dreary pool growing flatter and flatter. That's all there is."

The woman looked back at the man who was brooding away impassively. Dallow smiled. He had even surprised himself with his little speech. Pub philosophy, he thought.

"A good head," said the man without looking up. The woman looked at Dallow in admiration, anxious to see how he would react to this recognition. Dallow finished the remains of his whiskey.

"Are you a philosopher?" he then inquired.

The man now looked up for the first time and over at the woman, as if she had to decide.

"He's a construction foreman. Pipefitter," she said, "but he reads Schopenhauer."

Dallow raised his eyebrows, impressed. He looked around for the waiter, who was sitting at one of the tables playing skat with some guests.

"Do you know Schopenhauer?" the man asked without looking at Dallow.

"No." Then he corrected himself: "I once took a look."

"Read him," commanded the pipefitter.

Dallow promised he would. Again he signaled to the waiter, then asked: "You read only Schopenhauer? Nothing else?"

"What for?" The man was amazed. "There's everything there."

"That makes things a lot easier," Dallow replied amiably and took out his coin purse, since the waiter had arrived at the table. He paid and emptied his beer glass.

Then he asked, "And have you learned something from Schopenhauer?"

The pipefitter smiled and nodded, content.

"Have a good evening," said Dallow, getting up. He lifted his coat off the hook, put it on, and gave them both a parting nod.

The pipefitter looked at him and said, "I've learned that the straight way is the labyrinth."

Following this communication he and the woman looked at Dallow expectantly.

"Oh," is all Dallow said. He thought for a moment, again wished them a good night, and left the pub.

He went straight home as he was still cold. A few yards before his street he had to step off the sidewalk because it was torn up. The excavation was fenced off by poles and red and white striped tape. Dallow tried to peer into the black hole. A labyrinth, he thought, a peculiar philosophy for a pipefitter.

The next morning he was awakened by the doorbell. He stood up, reached for his watch, and went to the front hall.

"Who's there?" he asked through the locked door and heard a voice he couldn't understand.

"Just a minute," he called.

He went into the bathroom, put on his robe and combed his hair. When he opened the door he saw Schulze and Müller, the two men from the empty office in the District Courthouse. They beamed at him, cheerfully wished him good morning, and entered his apartment. Only after they were in the hall did Herr Schulze ask if they could come in. Dallow shook his head and said he wasn't up yet and therefore really couldn't receive any visitors, but both men assured him they only wanted to speak with him for a minute.

"All right, come in," said Dallow, annoyed, and he opened the door to his living room.

He offered them chairs and cleared glasses and dishes from the table. Then he wrapped himself in his robe and sat down with them.

"We've already been by twice, but unfortunately you weren't in," said Herr Schulze.

Dallow looked at him without replying. He heard the regular ticking of his old alarm clock in the bookcase behind him. He stood up, walked to the shelf, removed the clock, wound it up carefully and put it back in its place. Then he returned to his seat. The two men watched him.

Since Dallow was silent, Herr Schulze said, "We've come again to offer you work. Perhaps you've given it some consideration."

"Is that all?" asked Dallow. He stood up, walked over to the door and opened it.

"Please, wait a minute. Please sit down. We should talk," said Herr Schulze.

Both men kept on smiling at him, kindly, obligingly.

Dallow waited a few seconds longer at the open door, then said, "Please go. There's nothing I have to say to you, and nothing I want to know from you."

The men remained seated and did not stop smiling. Dallow was annoyed he had let them in.

"Please sit down, Herr Dallow," repeated Herr Schulze.

"Just go," repeated Dallow. Now he was getting loud.

Both men took pains to keep smiling, but their smiles faltered and slowly disappeared, leaving behind a pair of frozen faces. They stood up and went out through the door Dallow was holding open.

Without the slightest shade of friendliness Herr

Schulze turned to Dallow and said, "We can help you. But we can also make things difficult."

"I know," answered Dallow thoughtfully.

"We'll be in touch," said Herr Schulze from the hallway.

Dallow felt the cold air rushing in from the stairwell and shivered. He rubbed his upper arms with his hands and said, "That won't be necessary."

Then he closed the door. He went into the bedroom, lay down on his bed in his robe and thought about his unusual visitors.

He spent the day in his apartment. He leafed through his books and read old letters that no longer required any answer; their news and excitement only awakened vague memories and confusion. Distractedly, he prepared his dinner and ate it joylessly in the kitchen as he continued to go through his papers. His initial enthusiasm for cooking had subsided after only a few days, and he now performed kitchen tasks with his usual dislike.

That evening he went out. He walked irresolutely toward the streetcar platform and spent some time examining the schedule. When the first tram came, he climbed in, and once it pulled away he wondered why he had gotten on and where he wanted to go. He had no answer, but he stayed seated in the almost empty car and watched the young people who were standing in the front, fondling each other openly, shamelessly. Dallow observed that the girls were no less aggressive and brazen than the half-grown boys. The words they spoke to each other were few and repetitive, and many, Dallow noted with amusement, would have traditionally been considered grievous insults. But these young people took them unequivocably as signs of affection and appreciation. One of the girls kept trying to grab one of the boys between the legs, which he half tried to prevent and half allowed, proud and flattered.

Dallow was leaning forward. He stared at the young people in amazement. They noticed him, eyed him with hostility, and talked about him. Dallow could only make out a few words since he had quickly turned away to look out the window. He could sense the teenagers sauntering down the car in his direction. He forced himself to look intently out the window, paying anxious attention to the sounds behind his back. Suddenly his head was pushed against the windowpane. He turned around and saw a girl's face grinning. Her friends were lurking behind her. He quickly turned back to look out the window. He heard the young people pass. One of them leaned against Dallow's shoulder for a moment, but Dallow didn't turn around again. They're just children, he told himself, I can't let myself get beaten up by children.

Once the streetcar reached the center of the city, Dallow knew where he was going. He got off at the main train station, pushing his way through the people already climbing in. He crossed over to the station. In the arcade between the two main halls he searched in vain for an open store. Then he walked up the stairs to the tracks, but even the stands on the platform were closed. He went into the Mitropa, crossed to the counter, and waited for the man to take his order. He asked for a box of candy. The man nodded in the direction of the glass display box behind him containing packages of cookies and small boxes of candy that seemed covered with dust. Dallow shook his head.

"I was thinking about something else," he said.

"I'm always thinking about something else," said the counterman, not unfriendly. "It helps."

He returned to his sink. Dallow looked at the display case a little longer, then went outside and down the stairs. He had to wait a long time for the streetcar.

"I hope I'm not disturbing you," he said in place of a greeting when Elke opened her apartment door.

She shook her head and stepped aside to let him in. He, however, stayed where he was and looked her over. Very attractive, he thought, I like her.

He walked past her into the apartment. He was glad to notice that there wasn't any mattress in the hall this time.

"Come into the kitchen," Elke whispered and pointed to the open door.

"That's right," said Dallow, "is the child asleep?"

She nodded and put her finger to her lips. It's difficult, he thought, to start a relationship with a woman who just has a one-bedroom apartment and a child who is always sleeping in the only bed. He even thought of saying goodbye right away and leaving. The idea of a long evening in the kitchen made him nervous, the conversation with a lonely woman—who presumably felt neglected—an awkward kiss by the kitchen window, an unsuccessful pass at her near the stove while she's boiling water for tea. He would try to fondle her breast, to sneak his hand underneath her panties, and she would restrain him, undoubtedly by pointing to her sleeping child. Then she would ask whether that was the only reason he had come, which he would have to deny. He would again have to sit down, and after a few minutes the same game would begin again. Or else he would admit it, he would say that's the only reason he came, then she would be annoyed or sad or disappointed, and he would still have to remove his hands and excuse himself and comfort her, and the game would take a few more minutes to begin again. He sighed to himself. If he left at once he would save himself a long, aggravating evening, he told himself. But instead he went into the kitchen and sat down on the same chair he had sat on three weeks before.

The small television on the wooden chest was on, the table was littered with children's clothes, Dallow smelled food.

"I wasn't expecting you," said Elke, after she had

closed the door. She went to the television and turned it off. Then she removed the laundry from the table and tossed everything onto the wooden chest.

"Would you like something to drink?" she asked.

"I wanted to see you," he said.

She smiled sadly and stood in front of him. "You sure took your time about it."

"I was away," he lied, "I was away for a long time."

They sat across from each other and stared at one another.

"I really want to sleep with you, Elke," he said.

She looked at him intently and replied flatly, "I don't know whether I want to."

He nodded as understandingly as he possibly could.

"Tell me something about yourself," he asked her.

"I'm twenty-seven years old. I was married, now I'm divorced. I have a daughter. I work in a bookstore," she recited quickly and indifferently, sounding unintentionally like someone reporting official information to a bureaucrat.

Dallow laughed and asked about her daughter. He discovered that her name was Cornelia and that she was three and a half years old. He felt uneasy, and this feeling increased painfully when Elke told him it was now his turn.

When he mentioned that he had a doctorate, she simply said, "That would have impressed me ten years ago. Now I know it only means that your wife has to hammer nails into the wall without your help and repair electrical outlets all by herself."

Dallow laughed. "I'm not married," he corrected her, "but you're right, my scientific accomplishments are not very impressive. I was supposed to work in modern history, to burn the midnight oil discovering how illegal social-democratic parties managed secretly to print newspapers and row them across lake Constance a hundred years ago. And how the brave workers and artisans of Prague defended themselves against Windischgrätz's cannons with broomsticks and buckets of sand. But it's tiresome when science has nothing more to do than unearth anecdotes."

Then he told her about his arrest and trial and the time he spent in prison.

When Elke asked whether he was back at the university and he told her he hadn't worked since his release and still hadn't decided when and where he would begin, she gave a resigned sigh and replied, "I don't know what's wrong with me. But I'm always running into men looking for ways to avoid work."

When Dallow raised his eyebrows she added: "Two years ago I divorced my husband. I was fed up with having to keep him fed. I divorced him so I wouldn't lose my last bit of respect for him."

Dallow understood what she was trying to tell him.

"Don't worry. I'm used to taking care of myself."

"That's not what I mean," she said, "if that were all . . ." She didn't finish her sentence and looked him straight in the eye until he turned his head away and began staring at his fingers. She really is beautiful, he thought, a pleasant surprise.

"What are your plans?" Elke inquired.

Dallow kept staring at his hands, wondering what she wanted to hear him say. Then he looked at her and said, truthfully, "I want to sleep with you."

She smiled. "You're repeating yourself."

"I know," he said, "but in this case it's a pleasure to do so."

"Do you want something to drink?"

He nodded. She went to the refrigerator.

"One bottle of beer and one bottle of soda. That's all I have in the house."

They shared the beer. Dallow caressed the back of her hand with his index finger, softly. She did not object.

"And tomorrow morning you'll take off and show up again in another month—maybe."

Dallow inhaled and exhaled audibly and reflected. No matter what he chose to say now, it had to sound convincing.

"Don't be so sure," he finally answered, "I'm always good for a surprise."

He stood up, walked in back of her and placed his hands high on her breasts. He could feel her pulse and smell her hair and her skin.

"I want to sleep with you," he repeated quietly.

He felt a nearly imperceptible movement in her

body and waited anxiously for her reply. His hands lay motionless on her breasts. He tried to appear relaxed.

"But I'm not going to wake up Cornelia," she pushed his hands away and stood up. "Wait here," she said, then left the kitchen and closed the door behind her.

He heard her rummaging around in the hall and smiled once he realized what she was doing. He stood up, loitered in the kitchen for a minute, then removed his jacket, draped it over the chair, and untied his shoelaces. He listened to the noises in the hall, then heard footsteps going into the bathroom and the sound of running water. When he heard her coming out of the bathroom he turned to face the door.

"Come," Elke said quietly and placed a warning finger on her lips to remind him of the sleeping child.

For a moment she stood in front of him, naked, looking at him carefully, teasingly.

"You're beautiful, Elke" he said quietly, without moving.

She disappeared through the door. By the time he got up and followed her she was already lying underneath a blanket on the mattress behind the wardrobe, where the child had slept during his first visit.

"It's not very comfortable," she said as she used both hands to pull the blanket up to her chin.

Standing in the doorway, Dallow undressed rapidly and tossed his clothes at the chair in the kitchen. He stopped in front of her encampment and allowed her to look him over.

"Is there any room available?" he asked politely and pointed to the blanket.

Without moving she replied, "If you give me some time."

He lay down next to her, carefully. He could feel her arm and her thigh, and he waited. Some light from the kitchen fell into the hall. When Dallow turned his head toward her, he saw her eyes fixed on him in the half-darkness. They looked at each other without moving. When she put her hand on his shoulder he kicked away the blanket with his foot, sat up and studied her intently. Slowly he began caressing her, and he waited until he felt her body move before he knelt next to her and took hold of her, firmly, excited. He turned her body around, grabbed her breasts, her feet. He pressed his chest between her thighs. With his legs he pinned her torso hard against the mattress so he could feel her movements more distinctly, strongly. Without realizing it he knocked her against the wall, and he heard neither the dull echoing noise nor her quiet groaning. His hands slid up and down her body unceasingly, as if he were trying to hold and take possession of every wave and swelling of her skin, while her fingernails cut into his back and clawed wildly through his hair. And only after he rested his face on her stomach and kissed her thick nest of hair and she opened her thighs and lifted her lower body to press his head harder and deeper between her legs—only then did he submit to her hands and the rhythmic movement of her body until he felt that sudden, reassuring calm which left him weightless. He lay quietly upon her, without a thought, until she bit his hand, and he immediately closed it into a fist to lessen the pain.

When she let go he threw himself on his back. She breathed heavily, her eyes closed. Then she opened them, propped herself up, looked at him, and said, "Jesus, I think you broke one of my ribs."

Dallow rubbed the red teeth marks on his hand and replied, "I hope so, girl, because anyone who crawls into your bed better bring a teething ring."

He propped his feet on the wardrobe and sat up. He observed the bedding scattered between the door, the wardrobe, and the wall, shook his head, and said with amusement, "I don't know, but somehow it all reminds me of summer camp."

Elke pulled Dallow's arm out from under him unexpectedly so that he fell back on his shoulder. She placed his hand on one of her breasts. Then she sighed with pleasure and said, "How nice for you. My summer camps were a little less fun."

She lay over him, supporting herself in such a way that her breasts and belly barely touched his skin. She placed her head next to his and whispered into his ear, "Be still, think of the child."

And then she bit him, first tenderly and only with

her lips, then wildly and more and more painfully on his shoulder.

When Dallow woke up the next morning, Elke was standing in front of him with her daughter. The girl looked at him earnestly, keenly, and didn't take her eyes off him as he said goodbye to her mother. When Elke asked him whether he would be going away again for a long time, it took him a few seconds before he understood her question.

Before she left the apartment with her daughter, Elke said to him, "Sleep as long as you like. Then find some work."

"You sound like my mother," he replied. "Why is it that I always wind up with girls whose only ambition seems to be to sound like my mother?"

He heard Elke and her daughter go down the stairs. Then he stood up, went into the bedroom and lay down on the bed where the child had slept.

Around noon he left the house. He ordered breakfast in a tavern across the street. While he ate scrambled eggs and greasy browned potatoes, he listened to the workers who were leaning against the bar, drinking beer and talking loudly.

A newspaper was lying on his table. After paying and putting on his coat he returned to the table, grabbed the paper and stuck it in his coat pocket. As he walked past the bar and nodded goodbye to the proprietor, Dallow expected to hear some remark about the newspaper, but instead of returning his greeting, the man simply watched Dallow leave—as did all the workers.

He didn't open the paper until he was in the streetcar. He skimmed the headlines with disinterest and thumbed through the pages indifferently, without expectations. He realized it was the first paper he had seen since the day of his release. In his cell he had read the paper every day. They were distributed after work, and since the other prisoners were only interested in the sports page, he had always been able to take his time and carefully digest the news. He had never read newspapers so thoroughly and completely as during his imprisonment. The local news, the international section, the editorial page, the numerous speeches and the frequent announcements of awards and distinctions, the popular scientific articles, the extended weather forecasts—he read them all with the same detached attention. For him it was news from beyond the river, from a land he had once inhabited and which he had left long ago. Occasionally a familiar name of a street or building might stir a memory. Otherwise the news had no value for him; he read not for the sake of what was communicated but solely for the sake of the communication. He did it to fill his free time, and he quickly forgot everything he read, since he either didn't fully understand the meaning of what was printed or else he didn't care. He regretted that the daily paper wasn't devoted to some specific subject or another, such as minerology or the life of insects or else problems of gerontology. Though even that would not really have interested him; he would have read such a paper with the same indifferent, detached attention, but at least he would have had the feeling of slowly filling some small, not very painful gap in his knowledge.

He had only bought newspapers once since his release from prison, and—apart from the old papers he had found in his apartment—he hadn't read any. He noted apathetically the results of a referendum approving a new constitution, the same constitution whose draft he had studied so thoroughly in his cell, to the sarcastic comments of his cellmates. He examined facsimiles of documents that purported to connect the West German president with the construction of concentration camps during the Nazi era. And he read two short articles about Warsaw and Prague, from which he could only gather that the newspaper's editors were following certain events in these cities with great interest and deep concern, though what these events were remained unclear.

When he climbed out of the streetcar, he decided he would subscribe to a daily paper as soon as possible. Following his brief and boring perusal of the stolen newspaper, he concluded that one ought to read a paper every day. In his cell he had spent his most pleasant hours that way. Now, on the outside, he hoped the newspaper would provide him with a similarly mindless activity. He hoped it would help kill some of his abundant free time.

The next day he ran into Stämmler, his neighbor, and another short and meaningless conversation resulted, followed by a second invitation. To the surprise of both, Dallow promised to drop by. They arranged a visit for the following evening.

Then Dallow went to his bank, asked for his balance statements and spent several hours at home calculating every conceivable expense and bill in order to determine how many more months he could live off the money he had saved before his arrest. He kept jotting down new figures, adding them up, and then adding on to the total. In the course of the afternoon he convinced himself that the money would last less than a year at the present rate; he guessed his scant reserves would run out in ten months. At some point in his calculations he sensed that all his pedantic and ultimately useless arithmetic was just a pretext to avoid coming to terms with something. The numbers supplied specific superficial arguments for change, but they would never reveal the rudimentary problem: he was bored. The nerve-wracking days he spent in his apartment, busy with petty, superfluous activities, organizing his possessions, soon became unbearable. Since he began to fear the senselessly wasted hours, he got up later and later every day. In prison he had longed for this aimless and useless wasting of time, but now he had to admit that he wasn't cut out for it. He wasn't capable of doing nothing while watching the passage of real time; its slow, relentless loss caused him physical pain. The ticking of the second hand on his old loud alarm clock, which used to soothe him, now made him so anxious, he would break out in a cold sweat, unexpectedly, inexplicably. This would last only a few seconds, but it seemed menacing, and he read it as a dark omen. He often caught himself pacing around the room carrying an open book instead of sitting in the armchair, reading. And then he couldn't remember where he had stopped reading, when he had left his seat, or what he had just read.

He wasn't capable of doing nothing. He hadn't learned how, he told himself—even in prison he had worked hard, so hard that it annoyed the wardens, as he was pleased to observe. He had to confess that his attempt to outfox himself, to force himself to view inactivity as a new, enriching realm of experience had failed. He realized this with regret. He stood up, took the papers with their rows of numbers, and tore them into pieces. He had made a decision and felt immediately relieved, even though he still had no idea where it would lead. He had no idea what might open up, what possibilities might arise that were even mildly satisfying. He also didn't know what a middle-aged man could expect in starting a new profession, an entirely different line of work. So this is middle age, he thought, and laughed at the pathos the words contained, but quickly and superstitiously he added the counterthought: just the statistical middle of a life. He thought about his father and his father's wish that he return to the farm. He shook his head at the idea, but it saddened him that there was no going back.

He went to bed early so he could lie down and contemplate what possibilities still existed and which he should choose. Since he ruled out the university on principle he was soon at a loss. Up to now he had spent his entire life in schools and universities—apart from the two years in prison—and as a result he lacked the knowledge and perspective necessary to change his focus, to move away from institutions of learning toward discovering another suitable activity. He racked his brains without result. As much as he hated his inactivity, as much as it pained him, he also realized how much it still engrossed him. He realized that his confusion and lack of resolve were the immediate consequences of his current way of life—his aversion to getting out of bed in the morning, his unwillingness to think about the day at hand, and his unadmitted yearning for the evening, that time of universal relaxation, those hours when he happily left his house to mingle somewhere in the city with people who were recuperating after a day of work. For at that time, Dallow felt like one of them, even if only for those few hours. He had gained a freedom he could neither use nor even bear. This surprised and oppressed him at the same time, because he now knew that all the switches of his life had been set, by himself or others, and he could only continue running along the prescribed route, powerless to change a thing, incapable of surprising himself—even prison had not affected that.

He hadn't landed in prison for being criminal, rebellious, or courageous; he had been convicted and jailed on account of a stupid trifle, even if the sentence said otherwise and the judge was convinced he was right. Prison remained an accident in the steady trickle of his existence. Just an error, nothing more. A mistake on both sides. Nothing new. It had only been an interruption, and now that it had happened he hoped it would lead to one more final, important change of course. But he realized he didn't know how to take advantage of this opportunity, all attempts were useless, the event remained a regrettable and insignificant accident. Like a little electric train, he had been lifted off the tracks and now all he could do was make sure that the tiny wheels would be returned to their tracks without any further shakes and blows and in a condition good enough to pass the most stringent inspection, so that the little train could continue running along the endless loop, calmly, at a regular speed.

He was only thirty-six and already an old man, old enough at least to spend the entire day waiting to go back to bed.

Tomorrow, he said to himself, tomorrow I'm going to look for work. He laughed at himself, giggled, and pulled the covers over his shoulders. Then he thought about Elke. He wanted to sleep with her, but was afraid to visit her. He feared a steady relationship might develop without his having decided it and without his being able to change it in the future. But at the same time he knew that he would visit her again. Because the bars just bored him. The beauties of the night began to terrify him more and more, they made him feel disgusted with himself.

He would go back to Elke, and sometime, probably very soon, he would be deprived of this decision, too, he would only visit her because he had visited her one or two days before, and their being together would in reality only be the unending consequence of their once having met. They would make love in her bed or on the mattress behind the wardrobe because they had once made love there and would do so for the eternity to come. The little toy train, the model loco-motive named Hans-Peter Dallow, would continue along its straight yet looping tracks. Dallow fell asleep with a sneer.

Stämmler was surprised when Dallow rang the next evening. Dallow asked if he had come at a bad time. Stämmler assured him he had not and asked him to come in. They sat down in the living room. Stämmler poured two glasses of brandy. The conversation proceeded haltingly since Stämmler avoided talking about Dallow's imprisonment.

Dallow listened without helping him along, amused by the awkward detours around the subject of his confinement.

Half an hour later Stämmler's wife, Doris, appeared and asked her husband to say good night to the children. Stämmler asked Dallow if he wanted to see them. After all, he didn't even know the youngest.

Dallow was about to get out of his chair when he answered briefly and decisively, "No, I don't think so."

He saw that Doris was taken aback and added, "I can't seem to get anywhere with children."

The evening was torture for all three. Dallow asked Stämmler about the possibilities of finding work. Stämmler was loath to answer, at least that was Dallow's impression, judging from the man's monosyllabic responses. He explained to Dallow that there wasn't really much demand for historians in the world of commerce. When Dallow explained that he no longer wanted to work in his field but was looking for some other job, Stämmler said, "That's silly, Peter. Why do you want to throw away your education, all those years of work?"

Dallow looked at him seriously and answered honestly: "Because I don't have any time to lose. I feel I have to hurry."

And since Stämmler and his wife stared at him

without understanding, he added, "I feel it's time I finally grew up."

"That's right," Stämmler agreed, "that's exactly what I wanted to suggest."

His wife giggled shrilly and Dallow decided to smile in agreement.

"And where you work," he asked unperturbed, "do you see anything for me there?"

Stämmler shook his head. "You'd have to start at the bottom, way down at the bottom. That's no place to grow up."

Dallow looked at Doris and wondered whether she was still annoyed at his remark about the children.

"We still haven't said a word about the last two years," he then said. "Don't you want to know what our prisons are like?"

Stämmler and his wife exchanged glances. Then she replied: "We thought you wouldn't want to talk about it."

The answer surprised Dallow, he had to think about it. Finally he nodded his head and said, "You're right, there isn't really much to say about it. You live a very regulated life there, once you get used to it. And even that doesn't take very long. On the other hand, I did spend two years there, I can't simply erase it from my life."

"If you want to talk about it, please do," said Stämmler as he refilled their glasses, "we'll be glad to listen."

"No, I don't have to talk about it, I don't have any problems with it."

Dallow was annoyed and had answered sharply.

Then they were silent for a long while and when Dallow finally announced he should be thinking about going home, Stämmler only nodded and immediately stood up. They parted cooly.

At home in the kitchen Dallow drank another brandy and thought about his friends and acquaintances. He turned on the radio and listened to some sappy English hits; he sang along with their sweet, sad refrains.

Something had changed without his being able to tell precisely what. He considered getting together with some of the boys from the pen, but quickly discarded the thought. He wasn't friends with any of them, and he was sure none of them really valued his company. Although presumably he, too, would always belong, would always be subject to the prisoner's code, so abundantly articulated to him by the more experienced inmates.

Prison must have been more than an accident in my life, he told himself.

He noticed that he was talking out loud and pounding his hand on the table, unconsciously. That put him in a bad mood. He filled his glass to the rim and finished it in one gulp. The alcohol shook him. He stood up and peered into the small mirror hanging above the wash basin. He looked himself in the eye,

critically, and studied his face with suspicion. He realized he was homesick, deeply homesick in a way he
would not admit, homesick for his cell. He missed
that strange security, the comprehensive care, he
missed the total regulation of his life. In his cell he
never had to make a single decision. After he had exhausted his resistance against the fixed and incontest-
able regulations that governed every activity and
every minute of his every day and night, he not only
gave in to the accompanying freedom from decisions
but accepted it with a kind of satisfaction. And now
he missed the ordered daily routine and the instruc-
tions, he missed the thoughtless and decisionless existence that simply plodded on from one day to the
next. And perhaps the reason he couldn't climb out
of bed in the morning was because no one was bang-
ing at his door, ordering him to do so in a raw, unintelligible voice. I still haven't left my cell, he confessed
to himself, it looks like I have one leg in the pen as
well.

He poured more brandy and stared out the kitchen
window into the night. He could see the upper
branches on the tree in front of his kitchen, but not
the trunk, and everything further back was completely lost in darkness: the laundry lines, garages,
the tiny gardens. The dark kitchen window made him
uneasy. He had the ridiculous feeling that the night
was watching him through this window, that the window was one of the night's many eyes. Unflinchingly

he peered into the dark glass. He didn't dare sit with his back to the window. Tomorrow morning I'll buy some curtains, he said aloud, and drained his brandy. He was tired. Too tired to go to bed. Like a stray dog gone wild, he thought. He smiled at his comparison and thought about it for a long time. He found the image illuminating. Released prisoners, he told himself, are just like those miserable dogs: they're mangy, they're shaggy, they run through the city in constant fear of being beaten, searching tenaciously for something they do not know but nonetheless long to find. They're easily spooked and they bite and they're unpredictable, but still, they're only searching for a new master who will pet them and beat them and let them lick his hand, though inevitably they will bite that hand, either lightly and playfully or else with their entire unconsumed rage and deadly teeth, because they're still and forever searching.

Dogs gone wild, looking for a new master. Dallow thought about the women with whom ex-prisoners found refuge. They had to be domineering types with a lust for power, substitutes for lost security, the continuation of the prison's constant and complete providing. What the ex-inmates needed was the turnkey's familiar tenderness, the love of a sergeant fiercely putting their day in order, someone always ready to strike first to prevent an attack, a bite at his hand, someone upon whom they could rely without thinking.

He thought about Elke and wondered whether she was such a substitute for him, whether he was hoping to find in her the wretched security of the cell.

He noticed that it was becoming increasingly difficult to speak out loud. Supporting himself with both hands on the kitchen table, he pulled himself up, screwed the cap back on the bottle of brandy and walked over to the piano. He opened it, but was reluctant to touch a single key. He let the cover drop with a resounding boom. Then he went to bed. "What a charming evening, Stämmler," he said in a satisfied voice before he fell asleep, groaning heavily.

Dallow spent the next days looking for work.

He had decided to find a job as a truck driver. For a few years he had driven tractors and trucks in his village during summer vacations from school and later from the university; he had also passed the test for that class of driver's license. So he gathered all the necessary papers, climbed into his car, and drove to a canning plant in the southwestern section of the city. As the gatekeeper was writing out the visitor's pass, he read the list of current job openings tacked onto a wooden bulletin board. He asked the man how to get to the personnel department and walked over to the office.

He told the secretary why he had come. She listened without responding and then disappeared into the next room. When she came back she asked him to wait: someone would see him right away. He sat down and studied the dusty, yellowed posters that partially covered the cracked gray walls, exhorting all to follow the worker safety regulations.

He turned to the secretary and observed, "You must have a lot of accidents here."

She looked at him blankly. He pointed to the posters which she then examined—for the first time, so it seemed to Dallow. "No," she finally answered in a reproachful tone, then turned her back to him and returned to the papers on her desk.

Dallow gave up trying to start a conversation. Now he no longer liked her, he found her repulsive. He suddenly hated her. He hated her without reason, as he himself acknowledged, and only because she either wasn't willing or didn't have the time to have a conversation with him. She looked about his age; her most outstanding feature was a slender torso with large breasts all resting on a stocky, unshapely lower body. Even her arms and legs showed a similar asymmetry: her arms were slim and pleasantly rounded whereas her legs were unsightly and fat. As if two persons had been joined together, two puzzle pieces that didn't fit, or a figure from one of those children's books where you can mix and match heads, bodies, and legs in an endless variety of surprising combinations. Dallow shook his head in disgust: sympathy gave way to antipathy, and hate to an equally unjustified repulsion. He now hoped she would stand up so he could inspect her more closely. He wanted to see the stitches where the slender torso had been sewn onto the mismatched lower body. But she stayed seated on her swivel chair.

Dallow rose when the door to the next room opened and a man called out his name and asked him in. As he followed the man into the room, he turned around to look at the secretary. But she kept on working without even looking up.

The man closed the door behind Dallow, shook his hand and mumbled his name by way of introduction. Dallow understood it to be either Seidler or Seissler. The man asked him to have a seat and sat down behind his desk. He had light, thinning hair and an unhealthy red face. He asked the purpose of Dallow's visit and then inquired whether he had any experience as a truck driver. Dallow said yes and described his summer jobs in the country.

Herr Seidler or Seissler smiled: "And what was your most recent employment?"

"I just spent two years in prison," Dallow replied, trying not to seem embarrassed and making his voice sound calm, even.

The man behind the desk didn't seem surprised. He simply asked whether he might know the reason for the imprisonment.

"I played a song," said Dallow, "a tango."

Now Seidler or Seissler was surprised. He smiled at

Dallow, puzzled, and thought for a moment. Then his eyes narrowed and he asked: "A tango?"

Dallow nodded. "Yes," he said, "an old song. 'Adiós, muchachos, compañeros de mi vida'—maybe you know it?"

The man was confused. "And for this song you got two years . . ."

"Twenty-one months," Dallow interrupted, "to be exact."

"Was it perhaps the kind of tango that threatens the security of the state, Herr Dallow?" the head of personnel asked and leaned forward expectantly.

"That's what the judge thought," acknowledged Dallow.

Seidler or Seissler now smiled, satisfied and reassured. He leaned back and asked very ironically, "And do you still sing such songs?"

"I never sang. I merely accompanied this tango on the piano. But now I've even given up the piano."

The man behind the desk nodded approvingly. He took Dallow's papers and thumbed through the documents as he continued chatting.

"You really gave it up? That only reaffirms my opinion. Last week I was debating with my director whether imprisonment really can educate someone, change him, rehabilitate him and make him a better man. My director disagrees. For him the whole point of punishment is punishment, period. He doesn't believe in rehabilitation. He will be amazed when I introduce you to him. You find that strange, Herr Dallow? Listen, for a canning plant this is not a purely theoretical problem but a very practical one. Do you want to know what percentage of our workers are former prisoners?"

Dallow watched his I.D. papers trembling in the hands of the red-faced man. An alcoholic, he thought. What percentage are alcoholics?

"And before that you worked at the university," said the man. "As what? A truck driver? I can hardly read it."

"No, as a historian," Dallow replied, "first as a student, then on the faculty." And when he noticed the disappointment on the other man's face he added, senselessly, "Nineteenth century, beginnings of the workers' movement, that was my specialty."

The man dropped Dallow's I.D. on the table, annoyed.

"I see."

He grabbed the I.D. and handed it back to Dallow along with his other papers. "So why don't you apply for work at the university. We don't need any historians here. Maybe in three years when we celebrate our twenty-fifth anniversary. Then you could write our brochure. If you'd like to, come and see me in three years and I'll give you all the necessary facts."

"I'm looking for work as a truck driver. I no longer work as a historian."

"You mean you've given up your profession as well?

Imprisonment seems to have had astounding effects on you, Herr Dr. Dallow. My director will be stunned when I tell him about you. What else did you give up?"

"I'm looking for employment as a truck driver," Dallow interrupted curtly. "Could we please discuss that."

The head of personnel cleared his throat and smiled sympathetically. "No," he said, "I'm sorry. There's nothing I can do for you. At the moment we don't need any truck drivers. Please try elsewhere."

"But there's a job posted at the gate, clear as day," Dallow argued.

The head of personnel interrupted him. "That listing is no longer current. I'll have it corrected at once."

He stood up, went to the door and opened it. Dallow too stood up but remained standing in the middle of the room and asked, "And would you have something else for me? After all, you're looking to fill various positions."

Seidler or Seissler shook his head with concern. "I'm really sorry. We aren't looking anymore. We have all we need."

"How nice for you," said Dallow venomously.

"Yes," the man confirmed. "Good luck, Herr Dr. Dallow."

At the gate he once again looked at the wooden board and read the job descriptions advertised. He glanced at the gatekeeper and took a few steps in his direction. But then he turned around and walked out the factory gate without saying a word.

That same day he tried a toy factory and a whole-sale book dealer, but in both places truck drivers were suddenly no longer needed.

The next day it was already difficult to look up new places to ask for work. After three days he decided to call first to set up an interview and find out whether they really were looking for truck drivers. But when these efforts too met with the same rejections and he continued to be turned away with the same explana-tions—there was no opening, whatever he had been told on the phone was a regrettable mistake—the long treks and short conversations soon became un-bearable. He noticed how insecure he was becoming and how shyly he approached even the secretaries. He chided himself but he couldn't hide his insecurity very well. The more rejections he accumulated, the sooner he began to expect the next rebuff. The inter-views lasted a few minutes at the most, but afterwards he felt as exhausted as if he had labored the entire day.

By the beginning of his second week of job hunt-ing, Dallow was incapable of checking more than two places a day. Two days later even that was too much, and he returned home after the first rejection, where he then lay down and fell asleep at once.

He tried to find out why no one wanted to hire him, even though they all needed truck drivers and expressed a lively interest over the phone. But all he ever got in the end were repeated expressions of regret and excuses so lame they first annoyed him and later only added to his insecurity. It puzzled him that he couldn't find a reason for the constant rejections.

At first he suspected his imprisonment was to blame, but he soon discarded this thought, because whenever he voiced his suspicion during an interview, either bitterly and bluntly or even just by hinting, he would be overwhelmed with figures proving the contrary: not only did these employers have nothing against ex-convicts, but they actually were very interested in hiring them, they had very good experiences with them in the past. But unfortunately, and in contrast to what he had been told over the phone, at the moment there was no need for truck drivers.

Some days he believed he was the victim of a conspiracy. The peculiarities and suspiciously similar rejections and explanations seemed to support this thesis, but he avoided discussing it and attempted to convince himself otherwise. Nevertheless his mind frequently turned to Herr Schulze and Herr Müller. He guessed that they were involved somehow, but he was unable to bring his thoughts to any convincing conclusion. Besides, he feared he was beginning to detect in himself signs of a persecution complex, and so he tried to suppress such speculation.

.   .   .

Toward the end of April he gave up looking for work. He was relieved to wake up the morning following this nocturnal decision, freed from this despicable game of humiliations, excuses, and lies.

A shadow of worry clouded his satisfaction when he realized that his financial resources would be exhausted in a year at the latest, and that he now had even less of an idea what he would then do than he had had a month before. But a year's a long time, he told himself, and a lot can happen. Therefore the present worry is unjustified and foolish.

He thought about himself a good deal. Until now he hadn't realized how deeply the job search and rejections had upset him. Something had happened to him during these two weeks that he had managed to fight off in the two years of his imprisonment, energetically and successfully. But now these dubious, suspect, and unjustified rejections seemed to have destroyed his self-confidence once and for all. He felt sorry for himself, and although that was unpleasant and even repulsive, his defenses against self-pity were weak.

He thought about visiting Elke, but discarded the idea since he was afraid that his self-pity was also driving him to her. He didn't want a shoulder to cry on, he didn't want to be consoled.

He had to make it through on his own. He had seen her often during the last two weeks. Twice he had spent the night and slept with her on the uncomfortably short mattress between the wardrobe and the corridor wall. The next day he had gotten up with her and the child, had eaten breakfast, and left the house with them. He had talked with her about his job search, but she either didn't understand or else didn't believe his intentions were serious.

"If you want to work," she said, "why does it have to be as a truck driver?"

"Why not?" he asked back. "One job's as good as another."

"It's always the same thing," she answered while she was putting a coat on her child, "whenever men talk about their work you can see they have no intention of growing up."

Dallow gently massaged her back and the base of her neck as she was bending over her daughter trying to thread an arm through the sleeve of the coat, and asked, "Where's the difference? Do women talk about work differently?"

She pulled a woolen cap over her child's head and tied it down. Then she took the girl in her arms, held her in front of Dallow's face, and said, "That's the difference."

Dallow had hoped for some other answer, and in order not to have to reply he pulled them both forward and kissed each on the forehead. She's so wonderfully practical, he thought, why should I burden her with a problem that is impossible to solve.

He accompanied them to the streetcar, and as they

were saying goodbye, he promised Elke he would drop by soon.

"Call me at the bookstore first," she asked, "it's better for me if I know whether to expect the doorbell to ring in the evening."

On the day he gave up his search, Dallow went to Harry's café in the afternoon. He sat down near the bar, which was still closed, and ordered brandy and a coffee. He asked about Harry when the waiter brought the drinks.

"He's upstairs with the boss. They're going over the orders," said the waiter with a malicious grin.

Dallow looked around the café. As always, a few painters and instructors from the art academy were sitting at the round table behind the piano. They spoke loudly, smugly, and, as they brazenly sized up the women walking by, they frequently roared with laughter so raucous that the other guests in the café stopped talking for a few seconds and turned their heads toward the only round table in the room.

Dallow knew them from before his imprisonment. They came regularly, every afternoon between three and five, drank coffee and champagne at the table reserved for them, held court, made noise, and were generally popular with the waiters because they always left generous tips. It seemed to Dallow they enjoyed an enviable state of satisfaction both with themselves and the world in general.

He drank his coffee and brandy and ordered a second round. He waited without knowing what for. He had discovered a long time ago that sitting in a café was the simplest and most bearable way of waiting: the hours simply flew by, and with them that vague, crippling, and tormenting feeling of waiting for something that will never arrive because it doesn't exist.

An hour later Harry appeared in the kitchen door. He waved to Dallow and went to the round table to shake hands with the men sitting there. With his usual professional flair he spent a few minutes talking to them, slightly hunched forward, the fingertips of his left hand resting on the table. Then he went over to Dallow and sat down next to him. He made a few jokes, then called to his colleague and asked him to cover for him for a few minutes. The waiter grumbled but agreed and brought them beer. He also set down a plate and silverware since beer could only be served with something to eat; but an empty plate with crossed knife and fork provided a sufficient pretense to serve beer to regular customers.

"He's not going to last much longer," said Harry with a sad face. He was talking about his boss.

"The waiters and the cook are the only ones who earn anything here, the old man has to chip in. Now he's starting to cut back on the orders. That's the beginning of the end."

Harry downed his beer in one motion and lit a cigarette.

"In half a year at the latest," he continued, "he'll have to sell. He can't even pay our salaries on time, we only get installments. He's dead and doesn't want to admit it."

As he spoke he looked around at the tables; his eyes followed his colleagues darting through the room with their little silver trays.

"And what will you do when he closes?" asked Dallow.

Harry smiled, still watching the guests and waiters. "I just hope he holds out another half year, then I'm out of here."

Dallow waited until Harry looked at him. "Then you'll have your own place?"

Harry didn't answer.

"Was it very expensive?"

"You sure know how to ask questions," said Harry. He signaled to a colleague, poured the rest of his beer into his glass, handed him the empty bottle, and ordered another.

"October first I'm taking over an establishment out in Plagwitz. Good place for a pub. The present owner is over seventy. Everything's been taken care of." He grinned again.

"Are you going to run it by yourself?" asked Dallow.

"No. One woman in the kitchen and one waiter. But no crooks like the ones here."

"I happen to be looking for work myself," Dallow said casually, stirring his coffee.

Harry looked at him in surprise and thought a minute.

"I don't know," he said slowly, "but I don't think you'd last long. It's not right for you. I'd like to help you, but I need someone who knows how to get on with people. You're not really made for that, Peter."

He looked at Dallow with concern, apologetically.

"And what else?" asked Dallow. "How's the family?"

Harry drew his eyebrows together and made a gesture rich in meaning. His colleague brought a bottle of beer, opened it, and filled the glass. The waiter asked when Harry intended to change and go to work. Harry didn't answer, just stared at him and waited for him to leave. Then he said to Dallow, "Everything's fine, just great. And outside of that, it's the same old story. The usual complaints, you know what I mean."

He lit a cigarette.

"It doesn't add up," he said sullenly, "and in my opinion we're all being royally screwed by these women. Think about it, if we really are the incurable whoremongers that women always make us out to be, and if all of them are such loyal and selfless souls, then where the hell do the whores come from? Who do these male pigs get it on with? How come it's only the men who are constantly fucking their brains out? Because that's exactly what the women keep telling us. But the arithmetic is wrong, it's impossible. If all the men on this planet really are jumping into one bed after another, who's waiting under the covers? I mean, if we're all such polygamous pigs—which is what we hear day in and day out—then there can't be just one or two hookers in the world and everybody else is somebody's faithful wife—there's got to be a lot of women who are out for a good time as well. We're total dupes, victims of the scam of the century. But they take advantage of our bad conscience to convince us that we're the only ones who ever cheat. And that is mathematically impossible."

He finished his beer and waved to one of the tables. He looked at Dallow and asked, "What do you think?"

"I think you're right," said Dallow, smiling, "but at the moment that's not my problem. I've been out of the game for two years—it makes you see things a little differently."

"Believe me, we've been duped. They've succeeded in convincing us that we're the little pigs. They've got us believing it. It's mathematically impossible. But we have to live with the accusation. Science really ought to examine the question, it might help us all. Well, that's that."

He stood up and put out his cigarette. "I'll be right back, I'm going to change."

He pushed his way slowly through the tables, jovially, constantly on the lookout for friends to greet. And they returned his greetings enthusiastically, obviously honored by the attention of the head waiter. He disappeared behind the narrow door next to the piano. Dallow knew there was a narrow staircase leading up to the waiter's dressing room.

Harry reappeared ten minutes later. He was now wearing the same burgundy tuxedo as all the other waiters, along with a narrow bow tie and black pants. He smiled at Dallow and disappeared into the kitchen.

Dallow ordered his fourth glass of brandy and some lemon soda. He watched the change of clientele; the afternoon coffee drinkers disappeared, leaving their seats to more festively dressed couples, who asked the waiters for the tables they had reserved, presumably intending to spend the entire evening there.

An hour later the little band was playing dance music, and a few couples were slowly turning on the stone tiles underneath the stairwell. A few blue-collar types and their wives were now sitting at the round table that had previously belonged to the painters. The new group talked as loudly as their predecessors and made sure there was an equally steady flow of champagne. The bar, too, was now open. Dallow had nodded to Christa, the boss's daughter, when she came in. Later he had gone to the bar to buy some cigarettes, and used the opportunity to speak to her, but she was curt and distant. A factory manager from

Jena joined Dallow and unsuccessfully tried to start up a conversation. The man then sat down at the bar, from where he could view the entire café. There he was equally unsuccessful in his several attempts to ask women to dance. Dallow watched him, out of boredom. He had hoped to meet some friends, but he soon realized this was impossible. These friends belonged to his previous life, he had nothing to do with them anymore, nor they with him. This wasn't the same city he had left two years before. It was an unknown city with unknown people, and because he was not prepared to resume any contact with his former life, the gates to the old city would remain forever locked.

How little it took, he thought, to change his life. He kept looking over to the businessman from Jena, this small, rotund, and red-faced man who had obviously accomplished his day's work and was now determined to crown his excursion, this brief departure from his ordinary routine, with a little romantic adventure.

Harry came to his table. He didn't sit down, just stood in front of him, resting one hand on the edge of the table, and informed Dallow that he had suggested that his boss hire him as a piano player. Dallow thanked Harry but declined the offer.

"I haven't played piano for a long time now. That's all over," he said. And then he just shook his head while Harry tried to convince him otherwise.

Dallow felt himself slowly becoming drunk and asked the waiter for the bill. He turned back toward the bar. The fat man from Jena was now flirting with Christa. He must have bought her a glass of champagne, Dallow surmised when he saw them clink glasses.

As he stood up he saw Dr. Berger, his judge, walking in his direction. Dr. Berger greeted Dallow amicably, by name. He asked whether he could join him for a moment. Dallow nodded silently, he felt nauseous, his stomach was churning, and he made an effort to sober up.

"Thank you," said the judge, smiling.

Dallow thought a minute, but he couldn't figure out what the man wanted. So he waited without saying a word.

The judge kept smiling, which made Dallow nervous.

"It really was an enjoyable evening," the judge continued, "but I'm afraid there's something you still haven't understood."

He paused meaningfully. Dallow remained darkly silent as he tried to make sense of what the judge was saying and suppress the nausea rising in his stomach.

"You're still not right, not even in hindsight," the judge continued. "You were not the victim of any injustice, as I think you presently believe. Today's performance didn't prove that any injustice was done to you. The law is a living thing, constantly evolving. Just like society. And what's wrong can never become right. Wrong remains wrong, always, but everything is in flux, and you can never step into the same river twice. Justice did not serve you wrong, my dear Dr. Dallow. And today's performance, which really was very entertaining, only demonstrates that we find ourselves in a different year. The river flows, I'm sure you can understand that."

Dallow burped audibly and felt momentary relief. He now believed he was fully sober. He lit a cigarette and watched his fingers hold the match. They shook, and his hand hurt, and Dallow knew that the alcohol was not entirely to blame.

"I don't understand what you're saying," he blurted out. He tried to look bored.

"I beg your pardon?" asked the judge.

Dallow repeated: "I didn't understand one word of what you said. I don't have the slightest idea what you want from me."

"Don't get caught up in an *idée fixe*," said Dr. Berger, smiling with self-satisfaction. "You were wrong then and today does not make you right."

"I have to go," said Dallow. He stood up, supporting himself with both hands on the back of the chair. Once on his feet, he saw his lawyer also approaching, smiling. Herr Kiewer greeted him and shook his hand. He also thanked Dallow and said he had enjoyed the evening.

"I had a great time," he said, "I really laughed a lot."

"It certainly was entertaining," the judge agreed, "but I've just been trying to explain to Dr. Dallow that the performance in no way changes the earlier decision, neither in a juristic nor in a moral sense. Nor even politically."

"Of course not," Kiewer agreed, "but that's exactly what gives the show its special charm. It demonstrates that we have made some progress since then. And besides, that one number was truly funny, don't you think? Well sung, by the way."

He said the last sentence very loudly, since the musicians had resumed playing. Dallow put his hand on his stomach and pressed lightly to fight back the nausea that had again set in. Since Dr. Berger had also risen, all three men were now standing around the small table.

"I have to go now," Dallow repeated. His hand was still on his stomach.

"Good luck, Herr Dr. Dallow," said Kiewer, "and once again, thanks for the tickets. That really was a charming idea."

The judge nodded, just as benevolently.

Dallow thought about what had just been said. Finally he asked, "What tickets?"

He inquired hesitantly, indecisively. He hadn't understood a thing and was afraid he had misheard something.

"You sent Dr. Berger and me theater tickets, you

and your friends," said Kiewer and added, with annoyance, "have you forgotten?"

"I didn't send you any tickets," said Dallow.

"Of course you did," interrupted the judge. He began a thorough search of his suit pockets. Kiewer also
rummaged through the pockets of his jacket, and before Dr. Berger had found anything he pulled out a
letter. He removed a typewritten sheet from the envelope, unfolded and read it.

"Dr. Dallow's right," he then said, handing the letter
to the judge, "his signature is missing."

The judge also looked at the paper and returned it
to Kiewer. He apologized to Dallow for his oversight
and promptly took his leave, very formally.

As Kiewer too was about to leave, Dallow asked
him, "What kind of letter is that?"

Without waiting for an answer, he simply took the
paper from his hand and sat down to read it.

It consisted of only a few lines inviting Kiewer to a
performance of a cabaret in the Thomaskirchhof.
The letter carried five signatures. Dallow deciphered
the names of the five people who had made up the
student cabaret.

"A ticket was enclosed," said Kiewer, who also sat
down.

"What else?" asked Dallow in a hoarse voice.

Kiewer laughed. "It was your old number. The
same text that landed you all in the pen."

He leaned forward and said more quietly, "Dr. Berger didn't think it was funny, he was outraged. But I laughed a lot, really."

Dallow was having difficulty understanding him. "They were playing . . ." he said very slowly.

Kiewer interrupted him: "That's right, the same old song. Naturally I recognized it at once. Dr. Berger too, of course. Your friends were all sitting right in back of us. And they were enjoying it, you could tell. Why weren't you there, anyway?"

"I was only the piano player," said Dallow. Then he called the waiter and ordered another brandy. He offered Kiewer a drink, but the lawyer declined since Dr. Berger was waiting for him.

"I was only the tango player," said Dallow, staring at Kiewer darkly. "There's your proof that I was sentenced unjustly. With this letter in your hand you can reopen my case. I was only the tango player."

Kiewer waited until the waiter had left the table.

"Given today's performance," he then said, "we could of course try to reopen the proceedings. But apart from the legal problems involved, who would benefit? Do you really want to?"

"I would benefit!" Dallow cried out loud. "I would benefit! I was only the tango player!"

He finished his brandy and waited for his stomach to calm down. Then he tapped on the letter that Kiewer was still holding and said, quietly but with the persistent obstinacy of a drunken man, "There's your proof, Herr Kiewer. I wasn't even invited tonight. I was only the tango player."

Kiewer stood up. Dallow kept poking the envelope with his finger and repeated, "There's your proof. I was only the tango player."

"You're completely sloshed," said Kiewer disgusted. He turned around and walked over to where Dr. Berger was waiting for him.

Dallow gaped at him. With heavy, drunken movements he shoved back his glass and tried to stand up. Twice he fell back into his chair and grunted unintelligibly. Harry came to his table.

"Come on, Peter," he said. He helped him up and brought him to the coat room.

"Did you pay for everything?" he asked.

Dallow shook his head. "I don't know."

"I'll take care of it," Harry promised and helped him button his coat.

"Sleep it off," he said as he took him to the door, opened it and let Dallow out with a friendly pat on the back.

The next morning it took some time before Dallow could reconstruct the previous night, which he did not do gladly. He thought of calling Harry to find out what had happened, but discarded the idea because of the admission implied in such a question. He felt bad not being able to remember. It annoyed him because it made him helpless.

His apartment building seemed unusually noisy.

He looked up at the clock. It was eight. Then he listened again to the sounds in the building, the closing of doors, the latching of locks, footsteps on the stairs. For a few minutes he lay in bed and once more wondered what kind of work he could do, where he should apply. Undecided, he finally got up and went to the bathroom.

When he left the house an hour later, he noticed a newspaper sticking out of his mailbox. He removed it and quickly stuck it inside his coat pocket. He guessed it had been placed there by mistake and belonged to one of the neighbors. On the way to the garage, however, he remembered having subscribed himself. In front of the garage door he took the paper out of his coat and opened it up. He discovered it was Wednesday, the first of May; the front page was covered with large red and black letters and symbolic portrayals of red carnations. Dallow put the paper away and opened the garage door. He'd forgotten about this holiday and hadn't done his shopping in advance; he wondered what there was to eat at home. Then he drove into the city.

Most of the city center was closed to traffic. Dallow took a detour east, past the university clinics and the Alter Johannis Cemetery, then turned back into town at Marienplatz. He parked his car on the Karlstrasse and tried to get his bearings. He was looking for the home of Ulrich Klufmann, who, until two years ago, had been the student cabaret's director and chief lyricist. Back then Dallow had visited him two or three times: he recalled that Klufmann lived in an ugly and amazingly large apartment inside a completely dilapidated building. Now he had trouble finding it, since every building in the neighborhood seemed so dilapidated. He walked into one that stood off by itself. The right-hand door on the ground floor was nailed shut; to the left he saw a nameplate. Dallow switched on the light in the stairwell and looked in vain for mailboxes. He climbed up the stairs. The apartments on the second floor were uninhabited. One door was locked shut, but so broken down that Dallow could see into the bare, filthy rooms. He knocked on the door opposite and then opened it. Startled, he jumped back: the floorboards on the other side of the door were missing, and the spaces between the support beams were full of stones, debris, and garbage. Dallow went up another flight, holding on to the banister because some of the stairs wavered when he stepped on them. He heard music and saw nameplates on both doors. On the left he found the name he was looking for: Klufmann. He looked for a doorbell and then knocked loudly enough to be heard above the music.

Ulrich Klufmann opened the door wearing a bathrobe. He reached into his pocket, removed a pair of glasses, and put them on.

"Dallow," he said, surprised, "come in."

He walked in front of Dallow through the hall and

the messy living room, where the blinds had been let down, into the dining room. A girl in a trench coat was sitting at the round table, her feet resting on the porcelain ribs of a heating unit.

"Will you join us for breakfast?" asked Klufmann. He then said, "This is Theresa, my little Theresa. And this is my good friend Hans-Peter Dallow."

Dallow nodded to Theresa, who smiled in return. He examined the room, which was completely white with sparse but elegant furnishings—also white. Now Dallow remembered the apartment distinctly, the six or seven rooms surrounding a windowless kitchen. Klufmann had rented it for ten marks, because the building had been slated for demolition and officially closed to tenants. Klufmann had wheedled a lease from the owner and furnished the large apartment with valuable antiques that he and another student had bought from old widows for very little money. Dallow recalled that the two had founded a "five-mark club," whose one rule was that members could spend no more than five marks on any antique, regardless of its real worth. And by power of persuasion, charm, woeful laments, rumors, and occasionally even threats they managed to part the old people from their furniture for one or two marks.

"Make some more coffee for us," Klufmann said to the girl. He watched her as she walked into the kitchen.

"She's fabulous," he said to Dallow, "she does everything I've been dreaming about for two years."

The girl laughed out loud, looked at Dallow, and wiggled her hips before disappearing to make coffee.

"She's really good," Klufmann repeated.

"Do you want something to eat?" he then asked, and without waiting for Dallow's answer, asked, "How did you make out? I heard you were back. Feel's good, doesn't it."

Dallow only nodded. "I still don't have any work," he said finally.

"What's the problem? You want me to get you fixed up somewhere? Not too much work, good pay?"

"And what are you doing?" said Dallow, without answering Klufmann's question.

"I've become a writer," said Klufmann, giggling. "I write lyrics for cabarets. Freelance, but I see a nice, fat check at the end of every month. I played up the prison sentence a little, that helped. Somehow everybody's got a bad conscience, they feel it's their duty to help. You know what I mean. Anyway, I managed to get a pretty good deal."

Theresa came into the room, picked up the coffee pot, and poured the remainder into Klufmann's cup. The trench coat was too big for her, she had knotted it back with a belt. The upper part of the coat billowed out, revealing part of her breast. Dallow stared at her and turned red when he saw that Klufmann had noticed. Klufmann smiled at him with understanding and gave her behind a lusty grab. Theresa poured the last drops of coffee on his head and ran into the kitchen, quite pleased.

"I've already sold a few texts, new ones as well as old ones. And can you guess which was the first to make it on stage?"

"I already know," said Dallow. "An old, sad tango."

"Word's gotten around, I see. Now that was fun. For the third performance I invited our judge and the lawyer. Everybody was there, the whole group. Pure pleasure. And the judge was hissing. I made sure he sat right in front of me; he was white with rage and hissing."

"You're wrong. Everybody wasn't there," said Dallow very quietly.

Klufmann stopped suddenly and instantly understood. He slapped his forehead and winced.

"I'm sorry," he said, "that was dumb of us. We forgot to invite you. But I'll make sure you get a ticket, I promise. Just tell me when you want to go and I'll have one set aside. Or two. It's really stupid, but we just completely forgot. It wasn't meant badly, Peter."

"I was only the piano player."

"Don't be offended, Dallow. We simply forgot. After all, you were just standing in. You remember—Kreie couldn't make it, he sure lucked out with that operation. You just stepped in, that's why we didn't think of you. I'm really sorry, Peter. Forgive me. But it was just an oversight, not a crime."

"That's not what the court thought, Klufmann. I served the whole time. I wasn't in jail a single day less than the rest of you. In any case, the judge didn't forget me."

Theresa came into the room carrying a pot of coffee and a cup. Klufmann took the cup from her hand, placed it on the table in front of Dallow, waited for the girl to hand him the pot, and poured the coffee.

"Once again, forgive me," he said in a conciliatory tone, "I really am sorry. But up to the last moment I was so anxious to see whether the text would go through, it just slipped my mind to invite you."

"You were in prison too?" asked the girl as she sat down beside Dallow.

"I was only the tango player," Dallow replied amiably.

Then he asked her to pass the cream and sugar and concentrated intensely on his coffee. He noticed Klufmann and the girl exchanging glances.

"And what's your student cabaret up to these days?" he asked in the ensuing pause.

Klufmann laughed, relieved that Dallow had changed the subject. "Thank God that's finally over with. I'm twenty-six now, and that's too old to be working for peanuts. I want to see some serious rubles rolling in. I had to quit my studies; no more time for playing around. Got to grow up sometime. I want to be able to afford a bottle of decent cognac every now and then—that's not too much to ask, is it?"

Dallow listened in silence.

"And what do you do?" he asked the girl.

She giggled without reason and looked at Klufmann.

"She wants to go to school," he answered, "and until she does she's staying with me. I'm helping her prepare for the university."

Klufmann and Theresa laughed out loud. She clasped her hands behind her neck to calm herself down. But she kept on laughing, shrilly, until she got the hiccups and ran out of the room.

"Excuse me," said Klufmann, trying hard to keep from shrieking with laughter himself. He wiped his eyes and breathed deeply. Then he took the pot and offered Dallow some coffee. Dallow declined, drained his cup and rose to leave.

"You have it nice here," he acknowledged.

Klufmann nodded. And with some regret he said, "Some day they're going to tear this old heap down. I'll never have another apartment this big. And then what am I going to do with all the furniture. It takes up several rooms; after all, it's not just any old crap. Well, by then maybe I'll have gotten to know the right people. You know, nothing works like personal contacts."

He noticed the contempt in Dallow's eyes and shook his head. "No, my friend, you're wrong: I'm entitled to it. I've got a lot of catching up to do, two very long and very lonely years. And I'll catch up, you can bet on that."

Dallow merely said, "She really is a very pretty girl," and glanced at the door through which Klufmann's girlfriend had disappeared.

Klufmann squinted. "I hope you've found something for yourself as well."

Dallow nodded.

As Dallow was leaving, Klufmann again asked whether he should try to find him some work. Dallow declined the offer. He didn't like the idea of someone ten years younger wanting to find him a job—someone who only two years before was sitting in his class as a student, completely dependent on Professor Dallow. He didn't like it, although he knew a man like Klufmann could solve his problem quickly and easily, that whatever it was that kept causing him to founder, hopelessly, would be no problem for Klufmann. But in the end his terrible uneasiness won out, and Dallow was relieved to hear himself say, "Thanks. But that's not possible."

And when he noticed Klufmann's perplexed face he added, "You landed a job for me once already. I'll look after myself now."

As he went down the staircase, holding tightly on to the railing because of the loose stairs, he heard Klufmann call after him: "Let me know when you want the tickets. I'll see that you get them."

Dallow walked on down the stairs and didn't answer.

He sat in his car and laughed bitterly. He laughed at himself. Then he started the engine.

A few minutes later he stopped in front of Elke's building. When she didn't open the door he took a seat in the pub across the street, drank a beer, and waited. The room was slowly filling up with men returning from the official May Day parade who now intended to celebrate by spending the afternoon drinking. It soon grew loud, and cigarette smoke began to snake around the ceiling lights. The tables were empty, and the men were crowding around the bar. Dallow was the only one sitting and watching the street. As he fetched his second beer, he saw Elke and her daughter on the sidewalk across the street. He finished his beer slowly and went to the counter to pay. The bartender was rinsing glasses and didn't notice Dallow. The men with their backs to him were arguing loudly, excited by the beer and brandy. A young worker, a redhead, was speaking excitedly about Prague and Dubček. The bartender leaned over the counter, took the half-empty beer glass out of the young man's hand, and declared clearly and plainly, "In my pub there's beer and brandy and bockwurst but no politics. And that's the way it's gonna stay."

He cast a meaningful glance at Dallow. The men grew silent and looked his way as well. Then the bartender walked over, took his money in silence, and returned his change without a word of thanks. Dallow left the pub, making an effort to walk slowly and naturally.

He had his midday meal with Elke and little Cornelia and then accompanied them to the zoo. The girl refused to hold his hand, and scrutinized him keenly whenever he spoke to her or tried to touch her. He attempted to play with her and make her laugh, but the child remained mute and unapproachable. Dallow respected the child's reserve, he liked it, although he also found it annoying.

"Don't worry," said Elke, "she's used to being alone with me. It'll take time."

Dallow touched the child's hair with his fingertips and replied, "I'm afraid it will."

And upon noticing Elke's puzzled reaction he added, "I'm afraid that in time even she will lose her pride."

Elke laughed at him, took her child's hand and ran away with her. Dallow followed both slowly, with the happy smile of a self-satisfied family man.

That evening he proposed that Elke move into his apartment, which had one more room than hers and was better furnished. The offer confused her. She understood what he wanted to say and suddenly started fiddling nervously with the sleeve of her blouse.

"Let's not jump into anything," she finally said, glancing at him with a childlike smile. "I know how difficult it is to live with someone. Let's be grown-up about it."

She kept tugging the pleated cuffs over her wrists and waited for his reply without taking her eyes off her hands. Dallow was surprised. His offer had been on impulse, and he was so moved by his own magnanimity that her immediate rejection completely unnerved him.

"I'm getting old," he said, regretfully, "I remember times when I could have expected a different answer."

"Memories are the most beautiful thing about love," Elke remarked. She stood up and asked Dallow to sit in the kitchen while she put the child to bed.

"Say good night," she told her daughter as Dallow got up to leave the room. The girl clung to her mother, then ran unexpectedly to Dallow and kissed the astonished man on his cheek without saying a word, then rushed quickly back to her mother and grabbed her hand. Dallow was as embarrassed as the girl. He opened the door, then turned to Elke and said in a quiet but unmistakable tone of triumph, "I think you ought to reconsider."

"Please don't get sentimental," she replied, "Cornelia's just exhausted. She belongs in bed."

Two weeks later Schulze and Müller rang, rousing Dallow from his bed. When he opened the door and saw them standing there, he first slammed the door shut but then immediately reopened it.

"Come in," he said wearily.

He registered the surprise on their faces, then proceeded to the living room and settled into his armchair. He tucked his naked feet under his bathrobe, lit a cigarette, and, without asking the men to sit down, waited for them to do so.

"You got me out of bed," he said moodily.

"It's ten o'clock," replied Herr Müller.

Dallow looked at him uncomprehendingly. "As you know, I don't work," he said, "so I can sleep till ten if I like."

Herr Schulze laughed sympathetically and gave

Dallow an approving nod. He unbuttoned his coat and took some cigarettes and a lighter out of his jacket pocket.

"May I?" he asked Dallow, who nodded, bored.

Schulze studied the room as he lit his cigarette. Then he looked at Dallow, who was sizing him up in hostile silence.

"It's been three months since you were released from prison, Herr Dr. Dallow," he finally said. "Don't you want to work? Besides, this isn't just a private affair, my dear Herr Dr. Dallow. As you know, it's against the moral code and standards of our society not to work. There are very ugly words to describe that type of behavior."

"Parasite? Asocial element?" asked Dallow obligingly.

Schulze nodded and said, "Once again I'm here to offer you our help."

Dallow felt cold. He wrapped himself closer in his robe and readjusted it over his feet. Then he gave a long, loud yawn.

"You can forget about your offers," he then said, "they only annoy me."

He picked up the ashtray, slowly extinguished his cigarette, and said, "As you undoubtedly know, I have been trying to find work. But strangely enough without result. Wherever I went they suddenly didn't need workers anymore. The only reason I let you in my apartment was to find out why."

"You think we're behind it?"

"Yes."

Schulze leaned back and examined his fingernails. "You're wrong. Why should we have anything to do with it? How did you figure that?"

Dallow grimaced. "So why is it that I'm turned away wherever I go?"

"I don't know. Where did you apply?"

"Everywhere," answered Dallow, dissatisfied, "everywhere they were looking for a truck driver."

"A truck driver?" asked Müller amazed. And as if to add emphasis, he moved up to the edge of his seat. Dallow didn't pay him any attention.

"I understand," said Schulze. "I understand why no one wanted you. You're overqualified. Why should a factory hire a researcher as a truck driver? They don't want trouble. And when a historian with a Ph.D. wants to work as a truck driver, it smells like trouble. There's your reason. People have experience with applicants like you. Either they quit right after they start or else they want to discuss things instead of working. And who wants to ask for trouble?"

Dallow listened to him attentively. The explanation made sense, and he now regretted having asked, and having let the two men enter in the first place.

"So why do you need me?"

"You're a historian, with a specialty in Czech and Slovak history. We're very interested in that, especially right now."

Dallow interrupted him. "My specialty is the nineteenth century. Current events have never interested me. And politicians only attract my attention once they've started to moulder in the grave. They're a lot more honest then."

Schulze smiled.

"Don't trouble yourselves," said Dallow curtly. "What's going on in Prague concerns me this much." He snapped his fingers. "And anyway, I'm not a historian anymore. I haven't been for a long time. My last job was as a tango player, and in the pen I worked in the laundry. After a while you just lose interest."

"Maybe we can help you," said Herr Schulze.

"You can," said Dallow and looked him in the eye, "by telling me what it is I have to do to never see you again."

Schulze replied in a friendly, calm voice: "Nothing. If that's what you want, then you won't see us again. I just wanted to help you, that's all. You have my telephone number. Goodbye."

He stood up, cast a quick, admonishing glance at his colleague, and then both walked out of the room and the apartment so fast that Dallow had no time to get up or even answer.

For a moment Dallow worried that he might have been unfair or even hysterical. But then he shook himself quickly and started cursing aloud as he went to the bathroom to shave and wash up.

On Thursday he drove to Harry's café. He parked

his car in a nearby side street, right on the corner. He turned off the engine and the headlights, and as he was getting out he saw Kiewer and Dr. Berger coming out of the café. He didn't want to run into them, so he stayed inside the car. He watched them talk and say goodbye to each other twice—at least they shook hands twice. Then the defense lawyer took something out of his coat pocket and handed it to the judge. Other guests came out of the café and the two men had to step aside to make way for them. Their conversation was animated, and Dallow regretted that he hadn't left his car immediately and simply walked right by them into the café. Now it seemed too late, too odd to do so. He lit a cigarette. When he looked back at the two men they were shaking hands a third time. Then the judge walked right toward him. Dallow turned his head away and cupped his hand over his cigarette. The judge passed Dallow's car and stepped onto the sidewalk. Dallow now noticed that the judge's gait was strangely irregular: his right leg took slightly larger steps than his left. It reminded Dallow of a folk dance and he looked on in amusement. Then he got out, tossed his cigarette into the street, stepped on it, and locked the car. He glanced at the judge, who was gradually disappearing down the street, then at the café's neon sign, and finally back at the judge, who was now turning onto the Alter Amtshof. Suddenly Dallow buttoned up his coat and hurried after him. He was surprised at his own decision. By the time he reached the next corner, the judge had completely vanished. Dallow ran down the middle of the street for a few yards before it diverged. Behind him, in the distance, he heard a streetcar. He guessed that the judge had entered one of the buildings, but when he reached the fork Dallow regained sight of him. Dr. Berger was walking down Moritzstrasse, toward the Johannapark. Dallow slowed down. He tried to figure out why he had followed Dr. Berger. By the time he reached the park he was only a few paces behind him. The judge crossed over some grass to reach a little paved path that led through the trees and lawns. He turned around abruptly; he must have heard Dallow's steps, but then he walked on. Dallow thought that Dr. Berger had quickened his pace. Suddenly the judge stopped to let him by, but Dallow stopped as well.

"Do you want something?" asked the judge. He hugged his thin briefcase tightly, with both hands.

"Good evening, Herr Dr. Berger," said Dallow.

"Who are you?" The judge's voice seemed different now, anxious. With his right hand he let go of the briefcase and fished in his coat for a pair of glasses.

"My name is Dallow. We know each other."

The judge was relieved. He nodded several times, greeted Dallow, and turned around to go along with him. Dallow walked along without knowing what he really wanted from him.

"Did you want to speak to me?"

Dallow nodded. Then he took Dr. Berger by the arm and said, "Let's sit down a minute."

He led the surprised and slightly stunned man to a bench directly beneath one of the park lights and forced him to sit down. He continued to grip the judge's arm firmly.

"What can I do for you?" the judge said sharply.

He tried to move away from Dallow and nervously tugged at his arm, which Dallow was holding.

"Let me go, will you," he finally snapped and yanked his arm free. He looked at Dallow angrily.

"Why is it you sentenced me 'in the name of the people'?" Dallow asked.

He spoke calmly, without taking his eyes off the judge. He watched Dr. Berger's eyes move back and forth and then close slightly and he knew that the judge now thought he was crazy, aggressive, dangerous. Dallow quickly began speaking again to reassure the judge.

"Why didn't you sentence me in your own name, Herr Dr. Berger? Or in the name of justice, or the state? Why, of all things, 'in the name of the people'? You had no right to do that. You never asked the people."

The judge smiled reassuringly and gently placed his hand on Dallow's arm. "It's better if you go home now. We'll talk about it another time, agreed?"

He wanted to get up, but Dallow placed his arm over his shoulder and forced him to stay seated.

"Do you intend to keep me here by force?" asked the judge.

Dallow didn't answer. Confused, undecided, he pressed his fingers around Berger's neck. The judge suddenly gasped for air and his eyes began to stare dully into the void. A gust of wind hit the lamppost next to the bench causing it to creak. The judge began to choke with a loud, sucking noise. This hungry gulping startled Dallow more than the man's wide, protruding eyes. He quickly released his grip and slid down the bench a few inches away from the judge. He watched motionlessly as Berger sat there, shriveled and spent, like an old man trying to catch his breath.

"You're crazy," said the judge without looking at Dallow. He stood up. "You're crazy, Dallow."

Dallow remained on the bench, he heard the man's steps as he walked away and felt the cold of the May evening pushing against his body.

"All I wanted was an answer," he said aloud into the darkness.

Dissatisfied with himself, he stood up and walked back the way he had come. He went into the café, sat down at the bar, ordered a beer, and tried to forget every detail about the embarrassing event in the park.

.   .   .

For a few weeks he had been having difficulty getting up in the morning. Almost every day he stayed in bed until noon. He didn't sleep, he didn't read. He couldn't focus his thoughts, just passed the time in fruitless brooding. He kept thinking about prison: the doors slamming shut, the short loud commands, the odor of the cell. He forced himself to think about Elke. He was afraid to make decisions, he didn't want to tie himself down, he didn't want to ponder some vague future. At the same time, he was afraid their relationship could become something fixed and final, by sheer force of habit, depriving him of decisions. He thought about Klufmann living with a twenty-year-old girl. He had imagined something like that for himself, something small, uncomplicated, exciting, and entertaining that would someday end on its own, without tears. Dallow hated complications. A relationship shouldn't require long explanations and constant repeated assurances—but in Dallow's experience no woman was willing to forgo these endlessly twisting conversations. Including Elke. A girl like Klufmann's would suit him better, but he didn't want to put up with the naïve babble, the trivial secrets and excitements he no longer cared to share or even understood. He felt too old for that, it no longer amused him. Dallow was shocked to realize that he could be so rational about women. He knew he should simply fall in love, that that would be a solution, a rational solution. And he very much regretted that he couldn't use his reason to make that happen. Then he thought again about possible employment. The over-abundance of time paralyzed him. His infinite, end-less freedom was losing all structure, all consistency. Every day he felt himself sinking deeper and deeper into this great mushy expanse of time, with fewer and fewer prospects. He was afraid that one day he would simply dissolve. Finally, mortal fear drove him out of bed in a cold sweat.

At the end of May, Roessler called. He telephoned in the evening and asked Dallow to drop by the Insti-tute. Dallow responded curtly and crossly. He didn't have any reason to go, but he also didn't see why he should decline. He accepted, more out of boredom than curiosity. They agreed to meet the next morn-ing.

I have to get up early tomorrow, thought Dallow as he hung up. He felt he had betrayed himself.

That evening he met Elke at the bookstore. A friend had invited her to a birthday party and Dallow had promised he would go along.

He waited opposite the bookstore until she ap-peared. Then he crossed the street and said hello. He asked how things were going.

After answering him, she returned the question: "And what did you do today?"

He made a face and didn't answer.

They walked slowly through the old part of town; the traffic had subsided for the day. They walked in the park behind the opera and circled the small swan pond several times, since Elke wanted to. Dallow was careful to stick to harmless topics, and changed the subject whenever he was afraid he might have to talk about his future plans. He didn't have any, and he knew that no one, not even Elke, would accept that or even believe it to be true.

They arrived late: all the other guests were already at the table. Elke introduced Dallow to her friends and he shook everybody's hand. The women were friends of Elke, all about the same age, and all worked in the same bookstore. Two of them had brought along their husbands. They moved over to give Elke and Dallow room at the table. The hostess poured them some champagne, and they clinked glasses and wished her well. Elke hugged and kissed her; Dallow kissed her also, since she smiled and held out her cheek and seemed to want him to. Dallow noticed that everyone was furtively sizing him up. He turned to Elke and talked with her. The conversation, which they had interrupted, soon resumed. People were talking about Prague, the meeting between the Soviet generals and Dubček and Černik, and about the death of Masaryk, which was the subject of numerous speculations in Czech and Slovak newspapers, all of which the Soviet press indignantly rejected. One of the men wanted to know what Dallow thought and asked whether he thought Dubček had any chances of surviving politically.

"I have no idea," Dallow answered, "I'm not really interested."

He said it in a friendly manner, but it stopped the conversation and everyone looked his way.

"You can't really mean that," said the man who had put the question to him. "In that case you must be the only one in the whole country who isn't totally preoccupied with what's happening in Prague. One way or another we're all involved."

Dallow shrugged his shoulders to indicate his regret but did not respond.

"But you're a historian," said one woman, "Elke told me. I would think you'd be more interested than anybody."

Dallow gave her a friendly smile and corrected her politely: "I'm a piano player." And then he added, by way of explanation, "A tango player."

The woman looked at Elke in surprise, then back at Dallow and asked, "And where do you play? In a bar?"

"I quit," he replied, "I hung it up."

He imagined hanging up a piano and smiled absentmindedly.

"And what are you doing now?"

Dallow looked at Elke, but she could only return his gaze, questioningly.

"Didn't you tell them?" he asked.

Elke shook her head. Dallow thought for a moment and then said in a bored voice, "I'm writing a novel."

No one failed to notice Elke's surprise as she looked at her friend and started to say something, but then decided not to after all. The guests eyed Dallow with disapproval or bewilderment. The conversation now took some time to revive. Dallow was amused that no one spoke to him anymore.

They were now discussing writers, the proclamations of the Czech authors and the lengthy and polemical responses of a few East German authors in the local newspapers. Dallow stood up and studied the hostess's books, which lined the walls.

Later, as he was standing by an open window smoking a cigarette, the husband of one of the guests—the same man who had addressed him earlier—came over and joined him. They both stared out into the night, and then the man said suddenly, "I don't believe you. I don't believe you have nothing to say about what's going on in Prague."

"I know," Dallow replied. He carefully brushed some ashes from the window sill and watched a streetcar threading through the neighborhood, now appearing, now disappearing.

"After all, you're an intelligent man. Or are you afraid of speaking your mind?"

Dallow looked at him. The man was thirty years old, with fine, thinning hair and a slight midriff bulge. He was, if Dallow understood correctly from their introduction, an engineer. Dallow smiled condescendingly and said, "I just spent two years in prison."

Dallow's answer took the man aback, and in his astonishment he only said, "Well, so what?"

Dallow didn't respond. He ground his cigarette on the wall outside the window, threw the butt into the street, and rejoined Elke.

"Are you very bored?" she asked.

"No more than usual." He stroked her arm.

One of Elke's coworkers sat down with them and beamed at Dallow.

"Are you really writing a novel?" she asked.

"I'm trying to," he said, and looked at Elke.

"What are you writing about? What's your subject? Is it a love story?" she kept asking.

Dallow played with his wine glass and thought for a moment. "It's almost a love story," he stated. "The hero is an idiot, and in the end he gets what he deserves. That's it."

"Sounds great," said the bookseller sarcastically. "I just hope it's funny. People prefer books that are funny."

"Don't worry, it'll be a riot," Dallow promised. "They'll die laughing."

"Great," she said and stood up, "if it's that good, I'll sell a lot of copies. Just for you."

Elke took her hand away as soon as her friend had left.

"How can you treat people that way?"

Dallow didn't say anything. He just took a deep breath and let out an audible sigh.

"You're self-righteous and inconsiderate," she said quietly. "None of these people put you in prison. And I didn't send you there either."

"I never said they did," Dallow contradicted her sharply.

"You act that way. And not just tonight."

Dallow was silent. He knew he was wrong, and he didn't want to anger Elke.

"I'm sorry," he said, pained, and reached for her hand. "That's not what this is about . . ."

Elke didn't let him finish. "You have a problem, and you have to solve it," she said. "Don't come to me again until you've taken care of it."

He looked up at her, surprised. "You're throwing me out?" he asked, almost voicelessly.

"Don't get melodramatic," she said quietly and emphatically.

The next day he was at the Institute at nine in the morning. Roessler asked him to wait a few seconds. He rummaged through some papers on his desk, then went to the front room and spoke to the secretary. When he came back he sat down opposite Dallow at the little round coffee table. He asked how Dallow was doing with his work and made a face when he heard the answer. Then he asked him about his plans and shook his head in disbelief when Dallow calmly announced that he didn't have any professional plans. Roessler looked at him in silence, concerned, and Dallow waited patiently to find out why Roessler had wanted to see him.

Barbara Schleider came into the room with two cups of coffee. She gave Dallow an encouraging wink as she served him his cup.

"Will I see you again?" Dallow asked her.

"Whenever you like," she said in a voice full of promise.

Dallow watched her leave the room. Then he took out a pack of cigarettes but put them back right away when he saw Roessler's disapproving face.

"We are considering," said Roessler slowly, with gravity, "whether we shouldn't reemploy you."

Dallow was surprised. He put his cup back down on the table and asked incredulously: "Really?"

"How do you feel about it?" inquired Roessler.

Dallow considered. The offer was unexpected. He had thought he was through with that part of his life once and for all, but now the proposal confused him. He thought for a minute. Then he shook his head, almost imperceptibly.

"There's too much I'd have to forget," he said bitterly, "and I don't want to forget anything. I also won't forgive anything."

Roessler spread his arms wide. "I don't think you can find fault with me," he said indignantly. "I behaved completely correctly. Or are you reproaching me for becoming a full professor while you . . ."

Roessler didn't finish his sentence. Dallow only smiled.

"The prison sentence was stupid. The whole trial. But your performance wasn't exactly stellar. And it certainly wasn't very smart. But do we really want to talk about these stupidities?"

Roessler leaned back and looked at him with concern. Then he got up, went to his desk, opened one of the bottom drawers, and pulled out an ashtray. He placed it on the table in front of Dallow and said, "Only for you."

Roessler returned to his seat. Dallow was determined not to smoke anyway. He didn't want to make himself vulnerable in any way; above all, he didn't want to accept Roessler's gesture.

"Think about it," said Roessler, "forget all those stupid things and come back. You could take the opening for senior assistant. And in four or five years we could talk about a professorship. Naturally you'd have to apply for reentry into the party. But I don't think that would pose any insurmountable difficulties."

Dallow considered the offer. He thought about the eight years he had spent at the Institute working on his dissertation and then as an assistant professor. He thought about the discussions, the meetings, the committees, the amount of time senselessly wasted. He took out a cigarette, lit it, and stated firmly, "It would be like spitting in my own face."

Roessler looked at him, visibly worried. He rose and paced up and down the room. He leaned against one of the file cabinets and began to rock back and forth.

"As you like, Peter. It's just an offer. Think about it and let me know in a few days. I need your final decision by June fifteenth."

"It's already final."

Roessler went to his armchair and sat down. With a look of suffering he reached for a pencil and rolled it between his hands.

"I'll still wait until the fifteenth." And then he asked, annoyed, "What do you really intend to do? And what is it you're after?"

"No idea," said Dallow. And then he added, with a smile, "I really don't know."

"Excuse me," Roessler flared up, "I just don't understand you. What's gotten into you? Use your head, Dallow. What the devil is your problem."

"Everything's fine. Life gave me another chance, and I intend to take advantage of it."

Roessler took off his glasses and eyed Dallow closely.

He thinks I'm crazy too, Dallow was pleased to observe. He put out his cigarette and smiled as he added, "It never was my life's goal to become a senior assistant, Roessler."

Roessler cringed, then took his glasses from the table, put them on, and said in a bored voice, "Do what you want. But get a job somewhere. You could have problems."

Almost hostilely he added, "This offer wasn't my idea. It was—"

"Müller and Schulze," Dallow interrupted.

Roessler looked at him in irritation. "Excuse me?"

"I said, Müller and Schulze. Those two clowns—it was their idea."

Roessler shook his head, confused. "No. Dr. Berger called. The judge who presided over your trial."

Dallow stood up. "Was that all you wanted to talk to me about?"

Roessler didn't reply. Dallow nodded without saying a word and walked to the door.

"I'll wait until the fifteenth," Roessler said before Dallow left the room.

Barbara Schleider waved him over. Dallow sat on her desk and she offered him a cigarette. "Too bad," was all she said, and when Dallow looked at her she pointed to the intercom on her desk. "I heard every word."

"This Berger, was he here?" asked Dallow.

She shook her head. "He called."

Dallow was relieved to hear it. Suddenly, since her

smile was so inviting, he put his hand on her breast, without moving his eyes.

"Hands off," she said amiably. And since she kept smiling at him, Dallow was unsure how seriously she meant it. But then he quickly removed his hand. "Excuse me," he said, embarrassed, "It was just that I . . ."

"I know," she told him, "I know everything. Men don't have to explain a thing to me."

She laughed when she saw how red his face grew. In his embarrassment he asked whether he could take her to lunch. They agreed to meet downtown, since he didn't want to pick her up at the Institute.

When he reached the stairs, Dallow turned around and went back to the hall. He walked down to the very end, searching through the open rooms in hope of finding a former colleague. He asked a student about the first name that came to mind; the student only looked at him in surprise. Then he asked about Sylvia, but the student couldn't help him.

He walked the few yards' distance to Elke's bookstore. The women he had met at the birthday party came up and said hello. One of them asked about his novel. Then she went back to get Elke, who kept him waiting a long time. When she finally appeared, he was standing at one of the display tables, leafing through a picture book. He wanted to embrace her, but she wouldn't let him. She asked about his talk with Roessler, and he told her about the offer.

"What are you going to say?" she asked. And since

he hesitated in answering, she added casually, "Do whatever you want."

She had to work and told him goodbye. Dallow left the bookstore and walked downtown. He still had two hours before he was supposed to meet Barbara Schleider. He walked into a movie theater to see a film he had read a review of in a newspaper. There were only a few people in the audience—students and a few retirees. The students were talking loudly and didn't quiet down even for the film. Dallow felt disturbed by them, so he stood up and moved to one of the front rows, with the older people. As he watched the film he thought about the review. He was amazed at the way they had described it in the paper. An hour later he got up and left in the middle of the film.

Outside he was greeted by the warm May sun; the daylight hurt his eyes the way it always did when he went to a movie in the afternoon. He strolled slowly to the place he had arranged to meet Barbara, and waited at the door until a waiter ushered him to a table. He ordered a glass of juice, thumbed through a newspaper, and waited.

Lunch with Barbara was fun. She told him stories about Roessler and other colleagues and they both laughed a lot. When she brought up his present situation he answered evasively. But she seemed satisfied and changed the topic herself, much to his relief. She started talking about her boyfriend, a married professor with whom she spent weekends.

"I know about passionate love and I know about marriage," she said, "and all I ever got out of either one were sleepless nights and a few gray hairs. Now I spend two days with a man and have five days to recover. That's a happy mix, Peter, I think I'll patent it as a recipe for bliss."

Dallow nodded in agreement. "I like that," he said. "But it's women who are the problem. They aren't content with just two days, despite their experiences."

"Happiness doesn't just fall into your lap. It took even me a long time to figure things out."

Then she looked at him and added, carefully, "Believe me, men are a lot less sensible. Deep down they really just love themselves. And they only need us because the loneliness of their kind of love makes them anxious."

Dallow contradicted her without much conviction. Then he raised his glass, held it up to her, and said, "Actually, Barbara, we're the ideal couple."

She clinked his glass, drank down her own, and replied, "And that's the way we want to stay."

With these words she put down her empty glass, reached for his hand, which was caressing her upper arm, and put it back on the table.

"Don't look so forlorn," she said. "Maybe we are the ideal couple and maybe we're made for each other. But maybe not. Let's not risk finding out."

She smiled at him encouragingly, but Dallow didn't change his expression as he said, "I have the feeling you despise men, Barbara, and I'm afraid that that's the secret of your happiness."

She looked down at the half-empty plate and thought for a moment. "You're wrong," she said, "I don't despise all men. And there's even one man I love."

Then she looked at him and added, "But that's my son."

She spoke softly and sadly, and Dallow knew she was telling the truth.

"And I hope that he doesn't love me the same way," she continued, "because I wouldn't be able to say no."

Her confession embarrassed Dallow. To avoid having to reply he called the waiter and asked Barbara if she wanted another drink. She declined, and he asked for the check and paid.

On the street she took his arm, and they walked arm in arm up to the Institute.

"Say something," she pleaded when they stopped in front of the building. "I need your advice. That's why I told you."

He shrugged his shoulders helplessly.

"Did I shock you very much?" she asked, in fun.

"No," he replied very seriously, "but I don't know what to say. You'll have to come to terms with it on your own, Barbara."

"I know," she said, pleased, "and I promise you that in twenty years I'll have solved my little problem."

She hugged him, and to his surprise kissed him

passionately. Then she stepped back, took a kleenex from her purse and wiped his lips.

"I hope everybody was watching," she said and nodded toward the windows of the Institute.

In the door she again turned around and said lightly, "Forget it. Just forget it all."

Dallow watched her. He had the feeling that she gave her hips a playful swing just for him before she disappeared into the entryway and the large heavy door shut behind her.

He got in his car. Before starting it, he stared for a long time at a young couple making out in a phone booth.

When he opened his mailbox to take out the newspaper an envelope fell to the floor. He picked it up. It was a letter from the court, and the name Dr. G. Berger was typed over the line marked "Sender." Dallow thought about the evening in the Johannapark. The memory was unpleasant. He sat down in the apartment, placed the letter on the table without opening it, and thought. He reached for the newspaper and unfolded it, but he was too nervous to read anything. He took the letter, turned it over in his hands indecisively, and put it back down. The letter upset him greatly. He suddenly felt acid collecting in his stomach and stood up. He took the paper and went to the toilet. He spat several times, then sat down on the rim of the tub. He waited, afraid he might vomit. In the paper he read the official press releases about Prague, about the end of the meeting between the Soviet generals and Černik and Dubček, but the reports were brief and purposely vague, and Dallow had difficulty following them. An editorial criticized a West European government for suggesting that the Warsaw Pact intended military intervention in Czechoslovakia, accusing the paper of warmongering and malicious invention. The paper spoke of gangster methods and Goebbels-like propaganda. Dallow read the editorial carefully, hoping to find information that would help him understand the news items. Then he folded the paper and went back to the room. He tore open the letter. Dr. Berger demanded that Dallow visit him at nine-thirty the next morning. There were only two terse lines written in a gruff, commanding tone. The heading, too, was devoid of any formal courtesy: he was addressed simply as Herr Dallow.

Dallow's hands shook. He put the letter on the table and went into the kitchen to make some coffee. As he stood next to the gas stove waiting for the kettle to boil, he decided not to comply with the judge's summons. He went back to the room, took the letter, carefully tore it up, and threw it in the trash. He immediately felt relieved; even the unpleasant feeling in his stomach slowly subsided. He drank his coffee in the kitchen as he listened to the radio. The Western station was reviewing editorials from around the world. Here too they were concerned with Czechoslovakia, primarily Prague. It was mostly speculation, and Dallow was bored and started turning the knobs on the radio in search of music. As he regained his calm he realized that he had no choice but to comply with the judge's demand. He fished the torn letter out of the trash and furiously slammed the tin cover back over the bin. He looked for the snip of paper with the room number and stuck it in the upper pocket of his jacket. Then he left the house and drove to Lake Kulkwitzer to take a walk. But when he got there, he was too restless and climbed back into his car, drove onto the autobahn and circled the city. As he was driving he decided to visit Elke that evening and not say a word that would upset her. But when he reached the city he didn't drive to her place, but to his own apartment. He parked the car in the garage, ate a sandwich in the kitchen, and then went to the local cinema. Afterwards he went straight to bed, although he didn't fall asleep for a long time. He woke up twice during the night, having dreamt about his cell.

The next morning at nine-thirty on the dot he knocked on the door of the room indicated in the letter. A secretary answered and asked for the visitor's pass he had obtained from the guard. She went into the next room to announce Dallow's arrival. A few seconds later she came back and held the door open for him.

"You're still not working, Dallow," said Dr. Berger in place of a greeting. He was sitting at his desk, busy with an open file, which he held in his hand as he spoke to Dallow. His glasses were resting on the tip of his nose.

Dallow nodded and looked around for a chair.

The judge leafed through his papers. Then without looking up, he said, "That's not good for you, Dallow. Have my secretary give you the number, then call."

Dallow didn't understand what the judge meant. But he didn't say anything, he simply waited. Dr. Berger looked at his watch and explained: "Let's say three days from now. Call and tell us where you're working. It's better that way."

Dallow wanted to reply, but the judge cut him off. Without looking up from his papers he said: "You understand what I mean, Dallow. Don't forget to call my secretary. It's for your own good."

He leafed through his file, bent down over one of the pages, wrote something down, and then said, "You can go now, Dallow."

Dallow stood there, wavering. Finally he turned around and walked toward the door.

"That was attempted murder, Dallow. Do you know what that could cost you?"

"No," said Dallow strongly, facing the judge. "It was an unfortunate misunderstanding."

The judge looked up and sneered.

"Misunderstanding? What's that supposed to mean? Are you a coward as well?"

Dallow took two steps toward the desk.

"Let me explain," he said quickly, excitedly, "it's just a nervous disorder, a convulsive overreaction from prison, the doctor told me. It's slowly getting better."

The judge looked at him mockingly, incredulously. He shook his head and asked, "And does it happen often?"

"No, no it doesn't," Dallow hurried to say, "it was an unfortunate accident."

The judge's lips began to curl into a grin. He saw how anxiously Dallow was staring at him, hanging imploringly on his every word.

"That's an extremely dangerous illness, Dallow," he said sarcastically.

Dallow smiled as well.

"It mostly interferes with my piano playing. That's why I had to give it up," he said in a feeble attempt to make a joke.

The judge returned to his documents. "You should wear handcuffs," he said as he stared intensely at a sheet of paper.

Dallow stood in front of the desk, waiting silently. It was as if the judge had forgotten him. But after a pause that seemed to Dallow like an eternity, Dr. Berger said quietly, "Go."

"Thank you," said Dallow flatly.

The judge didn't look up. He waved his left hand in the air to signal it was high time Dallow left.

The secretary in the front room rose to meet Dallow. She signed his pass and gave him a small white piece of paper embossed with the court's address under which a telephone number had been written by hand.

"Thank you very much," said Dallow, turning red.

As he walked down the hall he was so relieved he felt he might be sick. He stopped in front of a window and pressed his forehead against the cool windowpane.

He never could have proved it, he mumbled to himself.

A woman carrying an electric coil for boiling water asked him if he needed help.

He shook his head. Then he turned to the woman and said, "How? How do you intend to help me? Do you have power, money, influence, connections?"

The woman clutched the coil to her breast and stared at him, confused and shocked.

"What's the matter?" Dallow continued, "you mean you don't have any of those things? So how do you intend to help me?"

The woman jumped back three or four steps without taking her eyes off Dallow. He could see she was frightened. Then she turned and scurried down the hall with short, quick steps. Dallow waited until she had disappeared behind a door, then walked on, pleased with himself.

When he reached the wide stone staircase that led outside, he suddenly turned around and walked down another hall, looking for something. He hesitated in front of one of the doors and knocked. But before he could turn the doorknob someone twisted a key inside the lock and opened the door slightly. A man—Dallow could barely see the tip of his nose—asked curtly and rudely: "Yes?"

Dallow muttered something about a mistake. He wasn't sure whether that was the same room where Müller and Schulze had taken him a few months earlier. He went out and surrendered his visitor's pass to the guard.

That evening he went next door to talk to Stämmler. Stämmler's wife let him in. She greeted him coolly, showed him into the living room and asked him to wait. Her husband was out shopping. She excused herself and left him there alone. Dallow sat down. In the next room he heard children's voices and the clatter of dishes. He looked around for a newspaper, then picked up one of the small bronze figurines standing on the table and studied it thoroughly. He was relieved when he heard the doorbell. He tried to make out the voices in the hall. When Stämmler came into the room, Dallow put the figurine back on the table and stood up.

"You have to help me, Jochen," he said as they shook hands.

Both men sat down. Stämmler offered Dallow some cognac and listened in silence.

"If I were you, I'd go back to the university," he then said, "that's the only advice I can give you."

Dallow shook his head. "That's impossible," he said, "I spent two years in prison."

Stämmler looked at him without understanding. "Well, so what?" he asked, disapprovingly. "What's your problem? They want you back."

Dallow realized that he couldn't make himself understood. He tried again: "That would be like signing my own sentence."

Stämmler looked at him without moving a muscle, then reached for the bottle of cognac and silently offered Dallow some more, which he declined. Stämmler filled his own glass, took a sip, and said, "Then you'll have to lug those two years around for all eternity. I can't help you."

Both fell into a stubborn, hostile silence that lasted until Stämmler's wife came in and asked her husband to open a tin can. He cut himself in the process and watched with interest as a small drop of blood formed on his thumb. Dallow stood up and said goodbye. At the door he said to Stämmler, "Sorry, I seem to have come to the wrong place."

Stämmler was holding his wounded thumb to his lips and sucking the blood. "It looks that way," he said, just as pleasantly, and then closed the door behind Dallow.

That evening he drove to Elke's, but she wasn't home. He went to the pub across the street, sat down at the bar and ordered a coffee. He watched the proprietor talk to some guests as he tapped beer and kept wiping the silver surface of the bar with a dirty rag. Without looking, he dipped the beer glasses in the sink, pushed each one twice against the round brushes mounted in the basin, turned them under the water and placed them beside the sink to dry. Only when he was drawing beer did he focus on the spigot while continuing to talk to the guests. He had thick, almost purple eyelids, and his neck and chin were covered with scars. When he noticed Dallow watching him he looked at him quizzically. Dallow shook his head defensively. The proprietor took three glasses filled with beer to the other end of the counter. He hadn't recognized Dallow.

An hour later he rang Elke's doorbell again, then drove downtown to Harry's café. He told his waiter friend that he was looking for work, any kind of job, and casually asked whether Harry could help. Only when Harry simply nodded and started speaking of vague possibilities did Dallow confess it was urgent. Harry hesitated, looked at Dallow searchingly, but didn't say anything. He promised to ask around and get back to him in the next few days. Dallow thanked him. He stayed another half hour and tried to start a conversation with the woman behind the bar, but she claimed to have difficulty understanding him, asked him to repeat practically every sentence, and responded only in monosyllables.

The next day Harry called at noon and offered him a summer job as a waiter on the Baltic. Dallow accepted at once when he heard that he could start in three days. He thanked his friend profusely, but Harry interrupted and told Dallow to come to the café the next morning, since there were a few things he had to learn. Then Dallow called Elke at the bookstore; they agreed to meet the next evening.

He took a suitcase out of the closet and began packing. He felt as happy as a child about to go on a trip who can barely wait for summer vacation to begin. He thought about the judge. He looked for the piece of paper that the secretary had given him and dialed the number. A woman answered. He asked if she was Dr. Berger's secretary. Then he said that as of the first of June he would be working again. The woman asked for his work address. He told her what little he knew from Harry. Since she didn't say anything more, he suggested that she tell Dr. Berger. He hung up, turned on the radio, and fiddled with the knobs a long time before he found some music he liked. Finally he finished his packing, closed the suitcase, and placed it in the hall. He tried to sit down with a book, but he was too restless, so he started going around the apartment preparing things for his absence.

He didn't want to spend the evening alone, and since Elke was busy he called the Institute to speak to Barbara. While they were talking he realized how senseless and misleading an invitation would sound. So he let it go. He looked through his little address book and paused at various entries, but then went on. He was afraid of misunderstandings and wanted to avoid stupid and possibly embarrassing situations. Finally he spent the evening cleaning his apartment and sorting the various food items he had stored. He was feeling good and twice walked over to the piano. He opened the cover, looked at the keys, and barely suppressed his desire to play.

The next morning he drove to the café. It was still closed, and Dallow knocked on the large glass pane. An elderly cleaning lady unlocked the door and let him in.

Harry was sitting upstairs with the boss; Dallow had to wait. When Harry came down he showed Dallow how to carry trays: a small tray with two cups of coffee and a large one with twenty filled glasses. Dallow had to carry and serve platters while Harry and the cook looked on and gave advice. Then Harry gave him the name and address of the inn on Hiddensee Island and suggested he call and ask what he should bring.

"Don't embarrass me," he said in parting, "after all, I'm the one who recommended you."

At home Dallow put on the black suit he had had made for his wedding years earlier and had hardly worn since. He looked at himself in the mirror. The suit was a little tight, the pants were no longer fashionable and therefore looked shabbier than they really were.

"You look like the descendant of a whole dynasty of waiters," he said happily to his mirror image.

In the evening he drove to Elke's. She was amazed when he told her about his new job and invited her to visit him on the weekends and to spend her vacation on the Baltic.

"That's no work for you and you know it," she said disapprovingly. "All you've done is find a hole to crawl into."

"At least it's a hole on Hiddensee," he said, "not a bad place to sneak off to for the summer."

They were sitting in her kitchen, the window was open and since the traffic had died down, they could hear birds twittering outside.

"And then?" asked Elke. "What will you do then?"

He casually shrugged his shoulders.

"You want revenge," she said bitterly, "and you'll end up ruining yourself trying to get it."

The child called and she went to the other room. Dallow turned on the television and straddled his chair to face it. When Elke came back she cleared off the table without saying a word and sat down next to him to watch a film. They didn't talk and didn't look at one another.

"Can't you forget?" asked Elke abruptly.

Dallow needed a moment to understand what she was getting at. "I don't want to," he answered without taking his eyes off the television.

"Do it for your own sake," she said, and since he didn't answer, she added quietly, "or for mine."

He looked at her, seeming to think it over. But all he said was, "What's the little one up to? Is everything all right?"

Later he moved closer to Elke to caress her. She brushed him off, but he soon made another attempt. She asked him to leave, but Dallow refused.

"Tomorrow morning I'm going to the Baltic and I won't be back for half a year," he protested, "it's my last evening."

He opened the bottle of wine he had brought. They drank without saying much.

"I meant what I said," Elke told Dallow as she got up and turned off the television. "Don't come back until you've solved your problem."

"But you will visit me, won't you?" he asked without responding to what she had said.

"I don't know. It doesn't depend on me."

He walked over to her, embraced her and unbuttoned her dress. She simply let it happen, and allowed him to do as he pleased, but she was distant and almost indifferent.

As they lay beside one another he suddenly sat up, looked at her, and said bitterly, "I don't want to forget anything, and I don't want to forgive anything either."

He stood up and got dressed. He parted from Elke at the door without kissing or hugging her.

"Goodbye," he said meaningfully, with an ominous face.

Elke gave a friendly smile. She seemed distracted as she returned his goodbye.

The next morning Dallow took another look at his packed suitcase and travel bag, went through all the rooms, carefully locked the door to his apartment, gave one of his neighbors the key to his mailbox, and drove off. Early in the afternoon he arrived in the village where his parents lived. He opened the gate and drove into the courtyard. The back door of the house was open, but no one was home. He checked both the sheds, and in the garden in back. Then he sat down in the living room and read the television guide. His parents showed up half an hour later. Some neighbors had recognized Dallow's car and told them. His mother went in the kitchen and reheated their midday meal for him. His father only asked a few questions, then went back out to the field. Dallow spent the afternoon alone with his mother. At five o'clock she left to fetch the milk cans from the drop-off point. An hour later she came back with her husband. All three of them went into the stalls to take care of the animals. Then they sat down to supper. His mother ate little, but she kept offering things to Dallow and went down to the cellar several times for some jars which she opened in the kitchen and served to her son. Dallow's father asked him about work. He explained that he would be working as a waiter over the summer. As he talked, he saw his mother gently stroke his father's hand in a gesture of reassurance. His father didn't ask any more questions. Shortly after supper they went to bed. Dallow didn't fall asleep until late. He was depressed by his parents' physical deterioration; he had forgotten how old they were. And he knew they wouldn't be able to keep the farm very much longer. It was an effort for them just to get around.

"This damned farm," he said aloud. Moodily he gazed out into the darkness.

Before his father left the house he came into Dallow's room, woke him up, and said goodbye. Dallow sat up in bed and shook his hand. Both men were ill at ease.

"Well," said his father. He nodded encouragingly to his son several times and left the room.

While Dallow was eating breakfast his mother sat down next to him and started talking about her husband's asthma. Dallow said that the nurse in the village clinic was no substitute for a doctor and that his father would have to visit a hospital in the city.

"Your sister says the same thing," said his mother, "but what am I supposed to do. He refuses to see a doctor."

Dallow looked at his mother with concern, but didn't know what to say. Awkwardly, he looked at the clock and said, "I have to be on my way."

His mother nodded and stood up. She went in the kitchen and packed some sandwiches and sausages in an old, carefully folded paper bag from the local store.

The Rügendamm was crammed with trucks, and Dallow could have walked more quickly than he drove. It wasn't until he reached the island that the roads cleared up. In Schaprode he parked his car in a large enclosed parking lot right by the harbor. A fat woman wearing a smock asked how long he planned to stay on Hiddensee.

"A few months," said Dallow.

"Then follow me," the woman said. She walked in front of the car and showed him where to park.

He got out, removed his luggage, and checked to see if all the doors were locked. Near the entrance to the lot he took a ticket and gave the woman some money.

"You will check on my car now and then, won't you?" he asked the woman.

She replied indifferently: "The parking lot is attended."

The ferry wasn't scheduled to leave for another hour, but some vacationers were already standing by the dock with their luggage, and Dallow joined them. Children were running all around, oblivious to their mothers' constant warnings. A small, pale man was missing a very important letter and he and his wife opened their luggage to look for it. The people waiting looked on in amusement at the small man's possessions spread out before them.

When the ferry docked, they were pushed back to make way for the arriving passengers. On the pier that led up to the ferry, a boatman started selling tickets. He asked Dallow where he was getting off and then named a price. Like the other passengers, Dallow put his luggage beside the gangway by the bow and climbed below. He found a place to sit in the stern. Next to him a local woman was talking to a young girl. She spoke in a husky, masculine voice and was so suntanned her skin seemed dried out. Dallow liked her dialect. He smoked a cigarette, looked out at the water, and tilted his head slightly to better hear her voice.

He disembarked at the dock in Kloster. A boy with a bicycle came up to him and pronounced his name tentatively. Dallow nodded. He placed his suitcase and bag on the folding luggage rack above the front wheel, took the handlebars from the boy, and said, "Let's go."

They walked up to the street and then followed a narrow path made of loose cement slabs that led to the fishing village. The road went up and down, and Dallow had difficulty pushing the heavily loaded bicycle. He really had to strain when he started climbing the sandy path that led to the higher part of the island. He tried making conversation with the boy, who looked about twelve years old, but the boy answered every question earnestly with a monosyllabic yes or no. Dallow stopped to rest in the little wood that stood before a steep overhang. The boy looked at him in surprise but didn't say anything.

"Do we still have far to go?" asked Dallow.

"That's it right there," said the boy and pointed to a house just in front of them.

Dallow shook his head in silence. He got up, took the bicycle, and shoved it another thirty or so feet to the entrance of the inn.

It was a large freestanding house with tables set on the terrace in front of the main entrance. A thin blond waiter sized up Dallow from the distance. Dallow removed his luggage, thanked the boy, and returned the bike to him.

"So, you're one of Harry's?" the manager asked Dallow after a brief welcome. "A good man," he added.

He looked about fifty and sported a small, clean-cut moustache. Next to his nose, on his right cheek, there was a dark red spot the size of a small coin, which he kept scratching. He asked Dallow for his papers and started looking them over.

"You're a . . ."

"I was," Dallow interrupted, bored. "That's all over."

"But in any case, you weren't a waiter."

"Just as temporary help. At Harry's," Dallow lied and looked the man in the eye.

The manager nodded. "I'll take care of your papers and get them back to you in a few days. Can you begin right away? We've already scheduled you for a shift."

"I just have to eat something first," Dallow nodded his agreement.

"Talk to Karla. She'll also show you where you'll be staying."

He stood up, crossed to the window and looked out.

"I hope you won't cause any trouble, Herr Dallow. Your predecessor wanted to get rich a little too quickly."

"I don't have that problem."

"That's what Harry said. Let's hope it's true." He turned to face Dallow. "Oh, and one more thing. For the time being, you'll have to share your room with one of your colleagues."

"That's not what we agreed," Dallow protested, "you promised over the phone . . ."

"I know," the boss replied, "but there's a shortage of rooms on the island. I'll do what I can. In two weeks you'll have your own room."

Karla showed him the little room containing two beds, a wardrobe, and two chairs. He threw his suitcase and bag onto his bed and opened the wardrobe, in which almost all the compartments were already full. The woman stayed in the room and watched. Then she took him to the kitchen, got him something to eat, and showed him around the house. She introduced him to the others. The sallow-looking waiter with thin blond hair who had observed Dallow's arrival was named Jochen Rose. He was the man with whom Dallow had to share the room.

The waiter looked at him with contempt. He didn't shake hands, and instead of saying hello he simply asked, "Do you fart in your sleep?"

"I couldn't say," Dallow answered quietly. From the minute he had laid eyes on him he had sensed he wouldn't get along with this man. He found him completely unsympathetic, and now he realized that the waiter hated him as well, without reason.

"I'll be able to tell you soon enough," said Rose, who then turned around and went over to one of the tables.

Dallow looked at Karla, who was standing next to

him, trying to suppress a laugh. He winced and they continued their tour.

In his room he unpacked his things and stuffed them into the remaining empty spaces in the wardrobe. Then he put on his old wedding suit and lay down on the bed. When it came time for him to start work, he went down and asked whether the headwaiter had arrived. He introduced himself and listened to the man explain the layout. He accepted everything the headwaiter said. He received a key to the strong box where the waiters' order pads were kept. Then the headwaiter showed him which tables belonged to which stations.

Dallow sat down in the kitchen and carefully read through the menu, noting the names and prices of the available dishes until the waiter he was to relieve appeared.

Dallow threaded his way through his tables. The season wasn't yet in full swing and it was quiet. His first guests were two elderly ladies with bluish blond hair who ordered coffee and liqueur and carefully checked the bill before handing him the money.

The next day he went to see his boss.

"You'll have to change my room," he said, "or I'm leaving. I haven't signed a contract yet."

The boss sighed. "It's always the same thing," he said, "no one even tries to be a little understanding."

He reached for the telephone and called a friend. When he hung up he said with regret, "It'll take two or three days. He promised me the room would be free but it's still occupied."

He inquired how Dallow was getting along with the work. Then he said, "Just stay out of each other's way."

"How can I stay out of his way when he comes back at night completely drunk with a woman just as plastered?"

"I'll talk to him," said the boss. But he said it without conviction, partly because he doubted the success of such a conversation, partly because he preferred to avoid unpleasant confrontations.

As he worked, Dallow was careful not to let it show that he had never in his life worked as a waiter. He did it for Harry's sake, but also to avoid condescending lessons from his colleagues. He watched the other waiters carefully, with the idea that careful imitation could compensate for his lack of experience. Whenever anyone called his attention to an occasional mistake, his reaction was arrogant and surly. He soon acquired the reputation of being a little unapproachable, but because of that his insecurities and lack of experience were overlooked. And that was fine with Dallow. He just wanted to get through the summer, to escape the restlessness he didn't fully understand and the judge's dark threats. That was why he had gone to the island, and he attempted—in spite of the work, which demanded a meaningless, routine civility—to preserve his old, tried and true solitude.

He had to share the room with Jochen Rose for

three weeks before he received his own equally tiny room. Their relations remained hostile. During Dallow's fifth night things came to a head. Dallow had again been awakened when the waiter returned to their room with a woman in tow, and in his anger, which was magnified by the late hour, he had cursed at them both. Undeterred, however, they climbed into bed and started making love. When Dallow felt the familiar itch in his right hand that always preceded that dangerous, inexplicable cramping, he stood up and pulled Rose—naked and surprised—out of bed and slugged him twice in the face so hard that he fell to the ground. Dallow then went back to bed and rolled over to face the wall. The woman, who had first screamed, was now just quietly whimpering. Dallow guessed from what he heard that she dressed, heaved the apparently helpless waiter onto the bed, and left the room. The next morning both avoided looking at each other. One of Rose's cheekbones was quite red. After this incident they never exchanged another word, but Dallow was also never again disturbed by Rose's ladyfriends.

Fifteen days later he moved into his own room in the attic. He wrote Elke and invited her and Cornelia to visit. She answered evasively. He repeated his invitation, this time more forcefully. But once again he had to wait two weeks for a reply, and then she said she couldn't make it before the end of August.

He spent his free time, mostly mornings, on the less

accessible northeast shore of the island. He always took some books along but rarely read more than a few pages. He had enough to do swimming and sunning himself. Or else he would watch the sea, the changing play of the waves, the eternal and eternally varied motions of the water. He never tired of these simple pleasures, and each day he waited till the very last minute before returning to the inn to put on his suit and begin his shift. He had every tenth day off. Then he would take the early ferry, retrieve his car, and drive to nearby towns to do some shopping. Or else he would look for quiet country roads untraveled by tourists and free from the gigantic harvesting machines. Then with open windows and a blaring radio he would race as fast as his old car could go.

More and more frequently, however, he chose to spend his free days wandering up and down the island. Twice he managed to cross over to the part that was posted as off-limits and walk down the Gellenstrom all the way to the Gellerhaken, thereby circling the entire island. He observed the rare birds, and took in, with similar detachment, the changing colors of the sky and its reflection on the water, and as fatigue began to overcome him, so did an overwhelming indifference. He was fascinated by the trees twisted so bizarrely by the wind. To Dallow, they seemed like creatures that had succumbed to some constant humiliation, and he was touched by the way they had found to live with their oppression. The straight way is the labyrinth, he remembered, and smiled. The phrase seemed contrived to him, unnecessarily grand. He looked out over the water and thought that in reality everything was much, much simpler. Then he went on down the beach, relaxed and satisfied, and crossed through the scorched heather, giving other strollers a wide berth. He returned to his lodgings at dusk, when the isolated houses and cottages lit their lights, and the heather grew dark and forbidding.

The work in the inn bored him, but he was kept busy and distracted and earned a lot of money, more than he had ever earned before. Experience was much more important than knowledge in this profession, and he soon grew used to his duties. The guests he waited on were almost always vacationers, patiently waiting for a table, then for a waiter to take their order. They were grateful for every friendly gesture and every joke. They were mostly elderly couples and lonely old women who strolled along the beach or hiked around the island during the day. The island's remoteness, its lack of bars and other entertainment kept away any visitors for whom the bare landscape, the narrow, stony beaches, and the incessant salty winds were not enough. There were only a few young people to be seen, some students and young couples who showed up with small children and lots of luggage and were constantly struggling with the catastrophes wrought by their offspring.

Sometimes the guests spoke to him, asked about his work, envied his long stay by the sea, inquired about available rooms. Dallow avoided making acquaintances and kept his answers friendly but evasive.

Twice he ran into people he knew. The first was a former student. Dallow saw him before the student recognized him, and so he was ready.

"Dr. Dallow," the student shouted, when he passed by, but Dallow went on without stopping.

The young man ran after him to say hello. Irritated by Dallow's dismissive bearing, he finally excused himself and muttered something about a remarkable resemblance. Then he again asked whether the man he was addressing wasn't Dr. Dallow from Leipzig who had been his instructor for two years. Dallow didn't answer, expressed his confusion and went his way. The student watched him, undecided, but no longer spoke to him.

One Wednesday Dallow spotted one of the two men who had kept harassing him in Leipzig. Müller or Schulze, he wondered. He went up to the table where the man was sitting with his wife and son and asked, "Müller or Schulze?"

"Müller," the man replied readily. Only then did he recognize Dallow and was embarrassed. With fidgety motions he reached for his cup but put it back down at once. He looked at his wife and then at Dallow.

"Good afternoon, Herr Müller," said Dallow with a friendly nod and left the table.

He didn't see Müller again. He was probably one of those vacationers who came to the island just for the day. They landed with the first ferry and then spread like locusts. They occupied all the establishments, crowded into the small village stores, took pictures of the lighthouse, waited in line for ice cream late in the afternoon, and positioned themselves along the dock ready to jump onto the ferry and grab a seat.

Dallow's small quarters were sparsely furnished, but even so, it was hard to move around since the furniture filled the narrow space. He bought a table lamp; the old-fashioned one on the wall illuminated the wallpaper more than the room and didn't provide enough light to read by. When he wanted to go to bed he had to shove the low table against the wardrobe in order to open up the sofa bed. The sofa itself was old and the green upholstery was so threadbare in places that he could see the stuffing. When Dallow pointed this out to Karla, who functioned as a kind of house factotum, she replied, "It sleeps two."

She said it without the slightest suggestion, as a simple fact, and Dallow didn't understand how that was an answer to his objection. But he soon found out what Karla was trying to tell him.

He made his first new acquaintance a few days after moving to the attic. Two female students were sitting at one of his tables and asked about a place to stay; they had missed the last ferry. Dallow regretted being unable to help. He joked with them and said he could only put up one of them in his small room. The girls giggled, paid and soon left. Twenty minutes before the restaurant closed he found one of them sitting again at the same table. Dallow recognized her and said hello, surprised. When he asked what she would like she said, "I'll take the room."

She smiled at Dallow, who took a moment to realize what she meant. Then he told her where to wait outside.

After they had closed the restaurant and cleared the tables, he looked for the girl and took her to his room. She undressed and washed up in front of him without the slightest self-consciousness. Dallow watched her with interest, still amazed.

"Did I surprise you?" she asked as she joined him in bed.

"Yes," he confessed freely, "but I'm prepared. After all, it does sleep two." He patted the sofa.

The girl laughed and said her name was Margarete.

"I like that name," said Dallow, "it's a nice name for a nice occasion."

He dropped his head to her breasts and caressed her.

The girl spent three nights with Dallow. Her girlfriend had also found a place to stay. When Dallow asked where, Margarete replied, "Let's just say, it's not as nice as where I am."

In the evenings both girls sat at one of his tables and let him wait on them and bring their food for free.

After he received Elke's first evasive response to his invitation to visit, he let more and more girls sleep over. It wasn't any trouble for him and he didn't have to talk fast or make moves to find a woman for his two-person sofa. He only had to not say no when asked about a room. He soon noticed that there were even girls who came to the island and sought him out. Their girlfriends had given them his name and address. Dallow was amused to function as a furnished room, complete with man. It even happened that he had to decline offers because his sofa was already booked.

He talked with the girls at length since their untroubled lightheartedness both attracted and irritated him. He didn't understand why they were immediately willing to go to bed with him just to have a place to stay on the island, he could only draw the banal and meaningless conclusion—at least it seemed so to him—that they belonged to a different generation. And he was not responsible, he told himself, either for the whole generation or for the individual girls. He enjoyed the pleasure of their bodies, so easily obtained; he grew choosy, accepting sleeping partners only upon thorough examination. And soon he stopped picking up the tab and always made sure that none of them stayed more than two or three nights. A few times he even let two girls spend the night in his room, but he soon had to give up that arrangement because one of the women in the kitchen who lived next door gave him a loud, indignant scolding. He avoided serious discussions with the girls. He loved to hear them talk about their lives and opinions and listened in silent amusement. He enjoyed their babble and their naïveté. If one of them tried to draw him out on a subject he would simply smile and stroke her reassuringly.

When Warsaw Pact troops entered Czechoslovakia in the second half of August, even the remote island was rent by excited and passionate debate as people discussed the constant stream of radio and television reports. When one of the girls asked Dallow for his opinion, he expressed courteous disinterest and at most a surprised amazement.

He heard about the invasion of Prague when he awoke early one morning, drew aside the curtain in front of the open window, and turned on the radio. A university student whom he had been putting up for two days was lying next to him, a very small young woman, somewhat plump. She listened to the news in disbelief. An announcer then read a communiqué from the TASS news agency. Dallow turned off the radio but the girl asked him to turn it back on. She listened breathlessly to the announcer and brushed Dallow aside when he tried to caress her. He was amazed to see her eyes fill with tears. He wanted to calm her down, but she wouldn't let him do that either; she stood up, went over to the window and stood completely still as the speaker on the radio read the communiqué in a flat, even voice. Dallow could see that the girl was sobbing. At first it amused him, but the longer he watched, the more extraordinary and moving she appeared to him. This half-naked girl with thick legs leaning her head against the window, crying, listening to an emotionless voice on the radio and wiping tears from her eyes as shivers jolted down her spine in almost even intervals—Dallow became aroused. He went to her, took away the sheet she was holding over her breast, and carried her to the bed. She just let it happen, and he made love to her while the radio announcer read a second heroic communiqué.

By the time she finally allowed Dallow to turn the radio off, the girl demanded that he say something. But he only shrugged his shoulders and asked what she would like for breakfast.

The girl wanted to leave for Berlin then and there to meet her friends. Dallow tried to persuade her not to go, to stay on the island one more day. Her tears had moved him, and he wanted to sleep with her one more night, but she just kept repeating that people had to do something.

"I can't understand how you can be so indifferent," she said, somewhat horrified.

"I'm just a waiter," Dallow answered her.

The girl protested. "You're a living human being, you're a . . ."

Dallow interrupted, objecting in a friendly voice, "Yes, and once I was a tango player. But that was a long time ago."

The girl felt he was mocking her and gave him an angry look but did not reply.

At noon he took her to the landing. After she had paid for her ferry ticket, he tried to persuade her one last time to stay on the island, at least for one more day. He was afraid she might do something in Berlin that would be dangerous for her or would cause her problems later on. Besides, the thought that this pudgy little girl was going to leave him, just when he was beginning to find her interesting and exciting was unpleasant. She silently declined his offer. Dallow was amused to sense that she now despised him, and again he felt an urge to sleep with her.

His relations with his colleagues worsened as the summer progressed. Since his room was in the attic of the inn, it was inevitable that everybody found out about his numerous ladyfriends. For unless he was willing to eat breakfast in his own cramped room, he had no choice but to take the girls downstairs—in full view of the cooks and waiters. The women in the kitchen inevitably made indignant, sarcastic remarks or accused him of seducing underage girls. Two of the waiters went even further and complained about Dallow's love life to the boss. One day he called both Rose and Dallow to his office and, embarrassed, asked for a little more restraint. But since neither one made any reply, he let them leave right away. Dallow didn't mind the talk or the reproaches; still, it was unpleasant to think that people mentioned him in the same breath with Jochen Rose. But he didn't say anything.

The only thing he did do following this conversation was write Elke asking her not to come. He did so because he was annoyed at her evasive letters, but also because he was afraid that his irritated colleagues might tell her more about his life on the island than he wanted her to know. He wrote that he didn't have any room for her and didn't see any way of putting her up even for a night.

On September third, Barbara Schleider called, joked with him a little, said something about changes, and hinted that there was something she couldn't tell him over the phone. Then she put Sylvia on, who wanted to talk to him.

She too inquired how he was doing. She wanted to know when he was coming back.

"Perhaps in one or two months," Dallow said, "I'm still not sure."

"And what will you do then?"

"Well, I really haven't given it much thought."

She said she had to speak with him and asked whether he could find her a place to stay for the next day.

"There's a bed ready and waiting for you," Dallow said.

Sylvia laughed. "That's not what I had in mind. I need a bed where I can get some sleep."

Dallow promised he'd take care of it, and told her where to find him.

The next afternoon she showed up at the inn. Dallow gave her an address where she could spend the night. They agreed to meet after his shift.

That evening they sat down at a table in the empty inn. They drank wine and Sylvia made fun of his waiter's uniform. Then she asked him if he would be willing to come back to the Institute as a full professor.

Dallow was surprised. "As a full professor?" he asked.

Sylvia nodded. "And it would be best if you could start in Leipzig tomorrow."

"And Roessler agreed to all this?" asked Dallow incredulously.

She smiled. Then she said, "I don't know. We didn't ask him."

Dallow said nothing and waited for her to explain.

"He had some bad luck," she said after a short pause. Then she explained that Roessler had been scheduled to lecture at seven A.M. the morning after the Warsaw Pact troops had marched into Prague. The lecture didn't begin on time since the students kept bombarding him with questions about the night's events. The professor hadn't heard the news and asked about the source of these rumors, and the students conceded that they had been listening exclusively to West German radio stations. Then Roessler declared that any news about an invasion of Prague was nothing but Western provocation. He said that military measures against Czechoslovakia, our ally, were absolutely out of the question and referred to earlier communiqués and commentaries from government and Party officials. The unreliability of these reports was revealed, Roessler went on to explain at length, in the claim that East German troops had also participated in the invasion. This report, he told the students, was particularly disgusting and outrageous, since it was unthinkable, for reasons of political and historical responsibility, that German soldiers could ever participate in an invasion of Prague. After the lecture a student brought him a daily paper with the TASS report on the front page. According to the students, Roessler read it and turned white as a corpse. Then he left the room without a word. He went straight to the university administration to report the mishap and admit his error. There he found out that they had already been informed about the incident. Six hours later he was suspended from his position.

Dallow shook his head. "I can't believe that someone like Roessler could trip up like that. He was always so smart."

Both smiled, lost in thought.

"I don't want to say it's weighing on my heart," said Dallow, "but where is Roessler now?"

"He's working at the Institute as an assistant. For the time being he's not allowed to lecture."

"That's still better than prison," said Dallow. He smiled with satisfaction. "And now you need me," he went on. He could hardly suppress the triumph in his voice.

Sylvia nodded.

"I'll give it some thought," he said.

"How long do you need?"

Dallow laughed out loud when he saw her looking at her watch. He promised to decide by tomorrow morning. They finished the wine, talked about Roessler and the university, and then he accompanied her to her lodgings. On the way he asked again about the pajama party of more than two years ago, but she just laughed at him and said she didn't know about any pajama party, he must have dreamed it.

Dallow fell asleep right away. There really wasn't anything to decide, and he slept peacefully and dreamlessly.

The next morning he went to his boss and asked for

an immediate termination of his contract. He explained that he had to leave at once for family reasons. Surprised, the manager hesitated, but signed the paper.

When Sylvia showed up at the inn, Dallow was sitting outside at one of the tables, packed and ready to go. He rose and walked toward her. She smiled happily when she saw his luggage.

"One condition," said Dallow, as she sat down at the table. He ran his finger along the top of an empty beer glass. Then he said, "No lectures at seven in the morning."

Sylvia laughed. "That won't be a problem."

Early in the afternoon they docked at Schaprode and climbed into their cars.

Just before Rostock they ran into a traffic jam caused by an army transport moving in the opposite direction. A truck running ahead of the transport signaled for them to pull over onto the shoulder and stop. Dallow opened his right door and turned up the music. He watched as the armored vehicles rolled slowly by. A light attack tank stopped thirty feet away from him; he could see the young soldier's face, made pale by lack of sleep. They're practically children, thought Dallow. He stared at the soldier, who seemed to have trouble keeping his eyes open. He imagined the boy losing control of the tank, he pictured the iron colossus suddenly breaking away and swerving right in his direction. The giant treads slowly rolled onto his little car, shattering the windows. The tank shoved the car forward, plowing it into a ditch, and then rolled on over. He saw his car caving in while he quietly sat inside, his hand cramped with pain, clawing the steering wheel until he was finally crushed, still smiling.

Dallow sat dreaming with open eyes as the army vehicles continued on their way. He had imagined the scene so vividly that he broke out in a sweat. He noticed that his right hand was shaking and he took it off the steering wheel, but it only took a few seconds before the shaking subsided; the cramp he so feared never came.

"That could have been it," Dallow said to himself aloud and rubbed his hand, "maybe it was my last chance."

When a second truck driver signaled the end of the transport, he waved to Sylvia, started his car, and pulled onto the highway. He was blinded by the September sun, already low in the sky, and drew down the visor. Two hours later they were on the autobahn, and Dallow accelerated, checking in the mirror to make sure that Sylvia's car was still behind him.

They reached Leipzig at seven in the evening. They used their blinkers to say goodbye. Dallow drove home, dumped his luggage in the entrance hall, turned on the television, and went to the bathroom to take a long shower. Then he opened a bottle of vodka and sat down at the piano. He had turned down the